They rolled off the couch,

narrowly missing the tiny liqueur glasses as they continued to wrestle. Cle finally managed to pin Dev to the carpet. Triumphantly, she looked down at him and saw his emerald eyes liquid with desire as he laughed with pleasure. "Gotcha!" she said.

"I surrender." Dev grinned up at her. Then, as her arms relaxed, his own went around her.

"Gotcha," he whispered, pulling her head down to his.

"You tricked me!"

"You know I'd do anything to hold you, angel," Dev drawled. In his kiss, Cle forgot the hard glitter that had shone in his eyes behind the words . . .

Dear Reader:

After more than one year of publication, SECOND CHANCE AT LOVE has a lot to celebrate. Not only has it become firmly established as a major line of paperback romances, but response from our readers also continues to be warm and enthusiastic. Your letters keep pouring in—and we love receiving them. We're getting to know you—your likes and dislikes—and want to assure you that your contribution does make a difference.

As we work hard to offer you better and better SECOND CHANCE AT LOVE romances, we're especially gratified to hear that you, the reader, are rating us higher and higher. After all, our success depends on *you*. We're pleased that you enjoy our books and that you appreciate the extra effort our writers and staff put into them. Thanks for spreading the good word about SECOND CHANCE AT LOVE and for giving us your loyal support. Please keep your suggestions and comments coming!

With warm wishes,

Ellen Edwards
SECOND CHANCE AT LOVE
The Berkley/Jove Publishing Group
200 Madison Avenue
New York, NY 10016

Second Chance at Love™

TORN ASUNDER

ANN CRISTY

A
SECOND CHANCE AT LOVE
BOOK

TORN ASUNDER

Distributed by Berkley/Jove

First edition published July 1982

First printing

Printed in the United States of America

Second Chance at Love books are published by
The Berkley/Jove Publishing Group
200 Madison Avenue, New York, NY 10016

TORN ASUNDER

CHAPTER *One*

CLE ORWELL STRETCHED and yawned, loath to open her eyes and start the day. She felt the warmth on her right side, the warmth that had become familiar and necessary in the short year she and Dev Carstairs had been together. Dev of the emerald eyes, whose warm gleam triggered a fire in her. Dev of the tall, broad-shouldered athlete's body which so excited her. Dev of the finely honed legal and business mind which kept her on her toes mentally and challenged her constantly. Dev of the midnight-black hair, not the blue-black of her own, but the night black of an Indian's with the persistent wave to it that no amount of brushing tamed. Dev of the six-foot-three-inch height and massive physique that made her own five-foot-ten-inch height and fine-boned frame seem diminutive. Dev who made every hair on her body feel curled, even to the hair on her head that was so straight it looked plumbed from crown to shoulder.

They had been together a year! She couldn't believe it! The anniversary of the day they had decided to live together would be in less than two weeks. Two weeks! Cle frowned, even as she lifted one hand to stifle another yawn. That's how long she knew Dev when she agreed to live with him. Two weeks of seeing each other every second they could, two weeks of having all her conceptions of a quiet bland love mutually satisfying to both parties ripped apart, two weeks of a shuddering, raw awareness that without him nothing would ever have the same dimension or color again. As the dawn was breaking after their first night together, the night that neither of them slept, Dev had whispered that he wanted her to stay with him, to live with him.

Did Dev remember that moment? Did he remember that night?

Cle swung her legs off the bed and came to a sitting position, trying not to be bothered by the thought that he might not recall those moments that were so precious to her, that were so vivid they might have just passed. She chided herself for being so stupid, being depressed because Dev might not—probably would not—remember the anniversary of the day they decided to live together! How Dev would laugh if she told him how daffy she was acting! She could hear him saying that. "Cle, darling, you're daffy!" he would say. Then, she thought with a pang, he just might tell her that he would leave her and go back to London where he came from. She shivered, angry with herself for being so imaginative. After all, she was a twenty-seven-year-old woman who had a very satisfying, however budding, career in design.

She remembered for a fleeting moment the young twenty-year-old Cle, fresh from the School of Design at Rochester Institute of Technology, coming to New York for the first time. She had been green as grass and scared witless when she applied for the job at Toner Fabrics and Design. She was still embarrassed when she remembered her stuttering acceptance of Jaime Toner's offer. It was exactly what she'd wanted: working in clothing design, not fabric design, with such a supremely talented, well-known person. She hadn't been able to believe her great good luck!

Her own innate shyness kept Cle in the background for the first few years, but gradually Jaime had come to recognize her talent and begun to give her more sophisticated assignments.

"What are you dreaming about? Come back under the covers and let me warm you," Dev's voice crooned in her ear as one of his arms snaked around her waist and pulled her back to him.

Cle smiled, her face turned away from him. "We'll be late. You have a conference call from Bonn today and I have to put the final touches on the fall show," she whispered teasingly, her body pliant in his arms as he turned her toward him, her own arms reaching up to feather the dark stubble on his cheeks. "You have to shave and shower. So do I." She laughed. "Shower that is!" She ran her hands up into his anthracite black hair, tousled by sleep.

"Yes, I know, but as much as I need to get a running jump on the day, I need to have you, too." He mumbled this into her neck, one hand running from thigh to hip to breast over her naked body. His mouth slipped down to her shoulder then fastened gently on her breast. The sucking and pulling sensation of his mouth drove her crazy . . . as he well knew. Her body turned liquid as he touched her. There was a fleeting moment of resentment, but before Cle could analyze it she was submerged in Dev again, drowning in that well of feeling that never seemed to quench the thirst they had for one another.

He played with her body as though he were composing a beautiful melody, and her form was the rare Guarneri on which it would be performed. With gentle awareness he probed all the recesses of her body that gave her the most pleasure. It never ceased to amaze Cle how devotedly Dev went about arousing her. Her pleasure seemed to be to him the most erotic thing in the world and one of his greatest joys in their love play.

But, then, she knew how much she delighted in pleasing him, too, and, as her fingers danced over him in the caresses he enjoyed, she felt ecstatic. Her rapture mounted when Dev's body arched in response to her touches.

Their blood pounded in tempo as their need reached incendiary stages. The silent explosion of their bodies was accompanied by their sighs and groans.

"Dev! Oh, Dev!"

"Cle, darling."

They were long past the time when they tried to check the flood of passion that engulfed them, and it was always so wondrous to Cle, so incredible. The intensity of the emotion increased each time they made love. It irritated Cle somewhat that Dev never seemed to be as affected as she was, that after, he was able to switch to "normal" faster than she could.

This time was no exception. As she lay breathing in ragged cadence against his neck, he was able to speak in normal tones. He let his hand move in a whorling motion down her spine and over her buttocks. "Cle, I know we've talked of this before, but I want you to rethink your position on my trip back to England. I want you to go with me."

"I want to go with you, Dev, you know that, but Jaime is getting the new line ready. With a little luck, I could be chief designer. I've waited for this chance, Dev, worked hard for it."

He rolled away from her and sat on his side of the bed, his back stiff. "I think I've heard all this at some time or other—"

"Then why don't you listen to me?" Cle argued, watching him rise to his feet and walk toward the bathroom. No matter how long they were together, how many years she knew him so intimately, she was aware that she'd never stop admiring his body: the long trim torso, narrow hips, muscular thighs, broad shoulders. She gazed at the light feathering of hair down his spine and remembered the tactile delight when she caressed him there. She hated to argue with Dev. He made the sun rise each morning for her. Still she didn't feel that she could back down on this. Too many times she put aside her own needs and wants in order to fulfill some request or need of Dev's. More and more, he seemed to demand her time, her energies away from her work. Cle knew she couldn't let him do it again . . . not this time. She had worked too hard for this chance.

She heard the bathroom door close with a muted slam and sighed, turning over on her stomach to bury her face in the pillow. It hurt so much when Dev was angry with her as he was now. Her feelings for him seemed to have ballooned out of all proportion, and it was getting worse. Even when she was hard at work on a design, his face would suddenly jump into her mind. She might be shopping for clothes on her lunch hour and find herself in the men's section of the store looking at a sweater that was just the color of Dev's lime-green eyes.

Cle was still lying there day dreaming when Dev returned from the bathroom, his hair glistening wet and curling, his face tight and controlled, the look that told her his anger was at full height.

"Are you coming to the Hopewell party this evening or have you something that can't wait at Toner's?" His clipped British accent was more pronounced when he was angry. At the moment he sounded like John Gielgud doing Hamlet.

"Of course I'm coming to the Hopewell party. We planned on going." Cle pushed herself to a sitting position, her eyes not quite meeting his.

"Say it out, Cle, for God's sake." Dev threw the towel to the floor with unaccustomed violence.

She glared at him. "Don't use that courtroom tone with me, solicitor. Your international reputation doesn't cut any ice here." In her agitation, she rose to her knees, letting the sheet fall.

The hard look on Dev's face softened, the sensual fullness of his lower lip more prominent as his eyes roved her body. "What reputation is that, darling? My bedroom one, I hope." His words had a softer slur to them, making Cle smile, even though that was the last thing she wanted to do.

"Never mind that now." She gave a reluctant laugh as he growled. She bit her lip looking right into those metal-green eyes. "Dev, I've told you before, that with the show coming up my hours would be erratic. Tonight Jaime wants to go over the choice of gowns for each model. I'll be as fast as I can. I won't come *home* and dress. I'll cut corners, taking my things to the salon. I'll just dress there and call a cab to go right to the hotel. I won't be too late." Cle held her breath while Dev stepped into a pair of gray trousers of the richest worsted that were tailored to hug his body like a glove. It was one of Cle's favorite suits and she loved to see Dev in it.

He didn't turn to look at her until he had knotted his hand-woven, deep blue and silver tie. "All right, if that's the best you can do. I'll meet you at the hotel."

The quick peck he gave her before he left the apartment told her more clearly than words that Dev was far from placated.

She stepped into the shower, sighing, the ambivalent feelings crisscrossing her mind. On one hand she was furious at Dev for what she felt was his high-handed treatment of her career and his lack of understanding. At the same time she felt a wrenching pain that they should quarrel so often about something that should have been so easy to handle. Why *wasn't* it easy to handle? And why *exactly* did they have such a problem working out such things? She'd asked herself these questions a thousand times; a thousand times she hadn't come up with good answers. And, so, she let the cold water course down her body until she was gasping.

Cle had to repair her makeup twice, her slight hand tremors betraying her tension. She knew that Dev would expect her to be wearing something black when she arrived at the gathering: Black was his preference for her at any function that included his colleagues. Dev was managing director of Hopewell, Brand, and Carstairs and, according to Silas Hopewell, considered one of the most brilliant in his field of international law and business.

As her hand was reaching for one of the simple black dresses in the closet, Cle paused, a mutinous look on her face. Turning from the closet, she reached into her lingerie drawer. She stuffed silky underthings into the canvas carryall that was like another arm to her. In it was her sketch book, her notes, swatches of fabric, and almost all the personal items that she considered necessary for her workdays.

By the time she had eaten her breakfast of a small bowl of bran with milk and honey, juice, and tea, she was having second thoughts about not bringing the black dress with her. "What if Jaime doesn't have anything suitable made up, stupid?" she muttered aloud to herself as she rinsed her dishes and set them on the drainboard. Mrs. Hubbard, the daily, would put them in the dishwasher but habits of neatness were a part of Cleora Orwell, plain, middle-class girl from upstate New York. She grimaced at her reflection in the gilded mirror in the hall, stifling the voice that told her to turn back and get that basic black dress out of the closet.

From habit she gave a quick glance around the ornate

foyer to see if she had left anything behind her. Not for the first time, she marveled at the richness of the entrance to Dev's apartment, the curving wrought-iron staircase in bronze leading to the second floor. A scant twelve months ago she'd never imagined herself living in such a place—never even thought to see the inside of one! Now it was her home, and had been for almost a year. She frowned at the shiver along her spine, then shook herself, checked to see if she had her key, then closed the door and walked toward the private elevator that would take her to the street entrance where she would catch her bus. Not all Dev's arguments and urgings had changed her habits of catching a bus to work and only in the worst weather would she take a taxi, when she was able to find one. The frugal habits that she was raised with were an integral part of her and something that Dev didn't understand but accepted with mocking tolerance.

The bus was late and so was Cle, not by much, but enough to keep her in a flurry of activity until most of the morning had passed. She had meant to ask her boss about a dress before he had worked himself into one of his emotional states that was the norm for a day in the life of the theatrical—but very talented—Jaime Toner.

Most of the models and modistes had gone to lunch by the time Cle entered the private elevator that took her to Jamie's studio. She knew that, as usual, he would be lunching on grapefruit and oranges plus a plate of English biscuits spread lavishly with crunchy peanut butter. Since most of his staff found his lunches appalling, Jaime generally ate alone, usually with swaths of material stretched around dummies or draped on couches and tables. Jaime would munch and stare, munch and stare. His studio was huge and—besides all the accoutrements of design—he had a sumptuous office adjoining the studio all done in pale blue with navy accessories. The wood fittings were oak and very British. Though Jaime had been born in

Brooklyn, educated in France, and had a Spanish mother, he was addicted to English decor and was fond of saying that his great grandfather was born in Sussex. Still, aware of all his affectations, he was lovable—and enviable. Jaime Toner was outrageously talented.

Cle looked around the cluttered studio, knowing from experience that—far from chaos—it was organized in the extreme: Everything was. She watched him now as he bit daintily into a wedge of orange and stared at a kaleidoscopic-colored silk draped across a chair.

"Jaime?" she called, her voice soft.

"Eh?" he glanced up, an irritated wrinkle on his forehead. He looked at Cle blankly. His brow smoothed as he recognized her. "Ah, Cleora, how did you know I had you on my mind today. Come in, come in. Join me for lunch."

Cle was sure that the fact she liked peanut butter was one of her most appealing characteristics as far as Jaime was concerned.

"I was talking to Brainerd this morning and I told him about the new line that I was thinking of starting and he told me that he is interested in beginning one himself. He asked me if I could recommend any talented person to him. I mentioned your name, dear." Jaime spoke kindly, handing her a cracker topped with a glob of crunchy peanut butter. With this he handed her a small paper plate with wedges of grapefruit on it and a neatly folded napkin.

Cle gave a resigned sigh. "I think you're about to tell me that I won't be the chief designer for the new line." She bit into one of the grapefruit wedges, the juice spurting toward Jaime.

"You won't get violent will you, Cle?" His voice had that funny squeak to it that Cle found amusing, but it didn't fool her. Jaime was very shrewd. He took a corner of his napkin and dabbed at the tiny marks of grapefruit that had landed on his smock.

"Why not me, Jaime?"

"Certainly not your talent, Cleora! You have a great deal of talent, dear, as you know. But . . . well, dear, you could use more seasoning. You need more experience in the public eye. Your instincts are still not honed as they should be. You will be chief designer one day, I'm sure, but not yet. As I said, Brainerd called—"

"I'm not about to go to Sydney, Australia, for my seasoning, Jaime, as much as I admire Max Brainerd's work. I would love to work with him, of course, but . . ." Cle shrugged and brushed at the cracker crumbs on her pink velvet corduroy vest.

"Ah, yes, there are other considerations are there not? The illustrious Devon Willett Carstairs, lawyer of international repute, consultant to the platinum set, wealthy patron of the arts, bearer of fine old name and title, the title which he does not use." Jaime gave her an elfin grin when she stared haughtily at him. "I've often wondered why he doesn't use his title."

"He considers titles useless in this fast world. Dev is a very liberal man."

"Yes, isn't he just?" Jaime asked, his tone sly.

It irritated Cle that remarks like that still made her flinch and, hard as she tried, she wasn't able to prevent the red stain rising up her neck. She rose to her feet suddenly, letting the napkin slide to the floor. Before she could turn away, Jaime took her arm in surprisingly strong fingers for such a flaccid looking person.

"No, wait, don't go, Cle. You know my stupid tongue. Please don't leave me. Let me tell you about the new line," Jaime urged.

Cle knew that in his own way he was apologizing. He absolutely never gave out information about a new line unless it was in the sanctum he called his conference room, a soundproof room that opened off his studio as did his office. Torn between her anger that he should have been able to strike at such a raw spot, her living with Dev, and her eagerness to hear what Jaime had to say about the new line, she hesitated.

"Please, Cle, I'll never make a remark about you and Dev again." Jaime paused a moment, a tiny frown on his face. "But you shouldn't mind remarks at this late date. You've been together a long time."

"A year. It doesn't matter. I still mind comments about us. I suppose I always will." She sank into her chair again and looked at Jaime in an inquiring way, hoping that he would take the hint and talk about the line instead of her and Dev.

Jaime wasn't too informative but he willingly talked of the fabrics he would be using, his decision to raise hemlines. When it came to the themes and shapes of the designs he would create for the season, he was more evasive.

Cle was stunned when Jaime rose and said that it was time to go back to work, that the lunch hour was over. She had been so absorbed that she hadn't noticed the time passing. She was leaving Jaime's studio when she remembered why she had wanted to see him. "Jaime, before I go, I have to ask you something."

Jaime looked at her, one sandy eyebrow raised. Not for the first time, Cle wondered how anyone with a Spanish mother could have such pale coloring. "What is it?"

"I was wondering if you might have a dress I could wear tonight." She pressed her lips together, feeling uncomfortable. "There's a dinner party for Dev's colleagues and business associates. He likes me to wear black . . . and I have a few good black dresses . . ." Cle cleared her throat.

"But you don't feel like wearing them, is that it?" Jaime looked at her, amused comprehension on his face. "You are such a quiet thing, Cleora dear, that probably Dev is like the rest of us. He doesn't realize how determined and independent you can be." Jaime waved aside any comment she might have made and stood looking at her, his face expressionless.

Cle stayed quiet, knowing from experience that Jaime was thinking hard. It was a mortal sin to disturb him in these moments.

"I think I have the dress for you. Young Mrs. Deerhurst's dress." At Cle's puzzled look, Jaime gave her an irritated glance and explained. "I thought I told you. After I designed it for her, I decided it would not suit her. She was very angry that I wouldn't let her wear it and didn't come to the salon for almost two weeks after our argument." He shrugged. "How foolish she was to think that I would sell her a dress that I knew didn't suit her. Silly female." He stood there, his fist pressed to his mouth. "Yes, this will suit you and I have accessories to go with it." He grinned. "You will be the sensation of the dinner party."

"Jaime, wait," Cle called to him as he left the studio and strode down the hall toward an even larger work area where many of the creations were locked away and much of the newly designed fabric was kept under lock and key.

Cle hurried after him, not catching him until he had inserted his key and was unlocking the door. "Listen, I don't want to wear anything bizarre . . ."

Jaime stopped so suddenly that Cle crashed into his back. "Are you implying that Jaime Toner would design anything that could be construed as bizarre?"

"No, of course not, but—" she gasped, a little out of breath and feeling frazzled. "Dev doesn't like me to be sensational. Well, what I mean is . . ."

"I know exactly what you mean. Devon Carstairs wishes to hide your light under a bushel for reasons that are known only to himself."

Cle let her breath out in a hiss. "Just what the hell do you mean, Jaime? If you're saying Dev is ashamed of me, trying to hide me, well then let me tell you you're all wrong. He isn't that way at all."

"Oh, I don't think he's ashamed of you either, but he certainly likes to play down your beauty. Perhaps he doesn't want you to try and compete with those exotic women his colleagues have in tow." He gave her a very irritated look, then held up his hand, palm outward. "I refuse to stand here and debate the merits of the famous lawyer from England. Do you want me to dress you or not?"

At the moment, Cle wanted to tell him to jump out the window. "Yes." She glared at the smirk on his face and followed him to the back of the warehouse-like room.

Again, Jaime inserted a key into a lock and they entered a room that was several degrees colder than the outer room. It took only a few minutes for Jaime to find what he wanted. Cle shivered as he shoved boxes into her arms. Then with Jaime leading the way and carrying the dress bag over his arm, they retraced their steps to his studio. Cle staggered a little. The boxes weren't heavy, just unwieldy.

In his usual autocratic tone Jaime ordered her to dress so that he might make any changes he deemed necessary.

"Jaime, I haven't time to try these things now. I'll do it later when the salon closes. I have to run through some sketches with Carr and I'm already late," Cle explained.

Without answering her, Jaime picked up the phone, barked some instructions, then slammed the receiver down on the cradle. "There, now! Will you be quiet? Carr will go over them with Danski and for heaven's sake don't tell me that she doesn't know about the sketches because she's your assistant and if she doesn't know, I'll fire the two of you. Now go. Change!" He sat down on a swivel chair and sent it skidding across the room. In moments he was immersed in the study of some silks that were strewn on a table.

It took two trips to the dressing rooms to cart all the

boxes and the dress bag. Cle glared at the concentrating Jaime, who seemed to be unaware of her existence as she struggled with her burdens.

She gulped with pleasure as she opened the first box and found silky lingerie that could have floated on air. Her eyebrows peaked in amusement at the peach colored sheerness of the undergarments, what few there were.

Curious, Cle ignored the other boxes and unzipped the dress bag, anxious to see the creation that Jaime was sure would suit her blue-black hair, a shade off the black that was Dev's. Her breath caught when she pulled the sky-blue silk dress from the bag. Very narrow squinned braid in navy blue outlined the crisscrossed bodice, the braid becoming a halter for the neck. There was no back to the dress! None! Cle began shaking her head "no" even as she put on the underthings and slipped the dress over her head. She didn't need to fasten anything, there were no fastenings of any kind. The bias of the silk made the dress hug her body like stretch fabric. Two pieces of material covered her breasts then came together at her waist to swath her body. The skirt was slit in front to the knee and with every move that Cle made the fabric swirled softly, molding her body. She looked over her shoulder and gasped. The dress was backless all right: it plunged to just below her waist. She twirled. It was a daring gown, but elegant and it matched her eyes to an incredible degree. Dev called her sky-blue eyes rimmed with navy around the irises "heavenly eyes."

She wrinkled her nose as she gazed down at the shoes that went with the gown. They looked a bit large. She slipped on the navy blue peau de soie sandals and adjusted the straps at the heels, happily surprised that they fit. The training she had had with Toner's made her swing into the traditional model's walk—hips forward, shoulders back, tummy tucked—as she glided out to Jaime.

He turned when she called to him, but did not betray his thoughts by a flicker of an eyelash until the slow smile began. "I was right again, of course. You will model that dress for me tonight. Tomorrow I will be inundated with women wanting to look like the lissome Cle Orwell, with the wet licorice hair that hangs like a curtain to her shoulders and the porcelain skin that looks like warm cream. My God, Cle darling, you are a beauty with those sapphire eyes. They look so mysterious with that rim around them. You're an angel from another planet, my dear." Jaime breathed, standing and taking her arm to twirl her around. "And you're my creation. You'll knock that assemblage on its collective ass," Jaime pronounced irreverently, making Cle laugh. He put his hand on her arm and leaned over to kiss her. "He isn't good enough for you, Cle. Give him up." Jaime muttered into her cheek.

She stood frozen, then leaned back, shaking her head. "If you mean Dev, Jaime, he really is good to me. I've been happy with him."

"He has also made you very sad. Do you think he will ever marry you, Cle? And don't give me that old saw that neither you nor Dev is interested in marriage. You know what I mean. He'll revert to family and the old school tie and, however much he says that it's out of date, he will decide that he needs an heir, that he must marry and continue the fine old name of Carstairs. Then *Lord* Carstairs will emerge and *Dev* Carstairs will disappear... and so will you from his life."

Cle laughed even though she felt a shiver of dread crawl along her spine. Jaime was saying out loud what had wriggled around in the deep recesses of her mind. Oh, not all the time, only now and then... when she was away from Dev for any length of time when he traveled or on the rare occasion when she did.

"Dev doesn't want marriage, nor do I," Cle said staunchly. "As to family, well, he has a brother, numerous cousins, nephews, what have you. If he were interested in heirs, he has them. But he is *not* interested.

Dev is a very modern man. I'm a very modern woman. We fit nicely."

"I repeat: he isn't good enough for you." Jaime swiftly turned the full force of his attention to the dress. "I don't think it needs a stitch of altering. You must wear only a pinkie ring and earrings with this. Your arms must be bare and so must your throat. Your lovely skin will be the best accessory. Do you have the jewelry?"

"I brought the sapphires that Dev gave me, but I don't have a pinkie ring. I thought I'd wear my gold watch . . ."

"No," Jaime thundered, "just the earrings then. Now get changed and get back to work. I don't pay you to loaf."

Cle shot a playful frown at him. "You're a slave driver and you know it!"

The afternoon proved to be chaos. Two of the lead dresses in the collection came up missing and the salon was in an uproar as Jaime threatened to behead the modiste who had seen them last. They were found in his vault. By regular closing time he had managed to reduce most of the staff to gasping hysterics and Cle's head was bursting. More, she was an hour late.

She tried three times to put on her makeup and though she was only wearing the lightest liquid foundation and a touch of blush, it took twice the time it ordinarily would have. Her eye makeup was blue shadow, the color of her eyes and her dark long lashes required no color or lengthening with mascara.

She heard the outer door of the dressing room open and called out to see who it was.

"It's Jaime. I've brought you something to wear over your dress and I do *not* want to hear your views on killing animals to provide coats for the wealthy. I have it on the best authority that these ermine committed suicide." Jaime studied her, the warm look in his eyes disconcerting Cle until she remembered that Jaime always appeared to be in the throes of passion when gazing at one of his creations.

"You have the look of a devilish madonna. You are at once restrained and wild, shy but flirtatious." Jaime's face changed again. "I think you have given me an idea for a new line. I'll call it . . . hmm . . . ah . . . yes, I'll call it 'Demons in Paradise.' It will be sensational of course!" Jaime stated, lifting the ermine to lay it across her shoulders.

The fur surrounded her neck like a cloud, outlining her face and the fall of black hair like a frame.

"You have never looked lovelier." He sighed. "I hate to see it wasted on Dev Carstairs."

Cle squealed when she looked at the time. "Don't worry, I'm so late, he'll probably be so annoyed that he'll ignore me all evening." Cle moaned, hurrying to the elevator and punching at the button, aware of Jaime behind her.

"Walk in as though you were royalty and very much aware that everyone there was waiting just for you so the party could begin. If that fool Carstairs ignores you, as sure as my aunt is a lush, the other men there will not!"

"Jaime, I don't know what your clientele would say if they heard you refer to your aunt in such a fashion," Cle scolded, laughing, as she stepped into the elevator.

He shrugged and lifted his hand in a farewell just as the doors closed with a whish and she was sped to the lobby area of Toner Fabrics and Design.

Hailing a cab in the cold rain was an impossibility at any time in downtown Manhattan and tonight was no exception. Cle tipped the night watchman at Toner's a few dollars when he stepped out into traffic and almost bulldogged a taxi to the curb.

By the time she reached the hotel she was an hour and a half past the time she had agreed to meet Dev. She hurried toward the dining room that the hotel clerk indicated, then stopped in front of the closed doors to take a deep breath. Dev would be angry. She decided to ignore that anger and be serene. At least that was what she told herself she would do.

Letting her breath go, she grasped the handle, pushed the door open, and stepped through, a smile pinned to her face. She let her eyes rove the room, willing her smile to stay in place as she saw how many people had left the cocktail area and were now seated. It unnerved her as a herd of sleek heads turned in her direction. She knew with a sinking feeling that it would seem to some as if she had deliberately timed her entrance. Biting her lip, she whispered, "To hell with them," and continued to look for Dev.

The hair raising on her arms was the first signal that he was near her. She turned, her smile in place, looking at a spot over his left shoulder. "Hello. Sorry I'm late. Things were wild this afternoon."

"Of course. At my place it was much different. We just sat around napping or chatting." His British accent was clipped. As he lifted the swath of ermine from her shoulders his eyes narrowed on the fur. He was still looking at it when he spoke again, the measured words in even softer tones and telling her he was *very* angry! "I can't remember the number of times you told me never to buy you a fur. That you didn't believe . . ." He turned to look at her, the faintest widening of his eyes, the trailing voice, the muscle jumping at the corner of his mouth, telling her of his feelings more than words could.

Cle swallowed when she looked up into the leaping green eyes. "I know you like me in blue, so I wore one of Jaime's new creations." She cleared her throat over the lie. "Do you like it?"

"Every man here will like it on you." His teeth snapped together, the pallor of his face more pronounced as his hand reaching round her back encountered her skin. "What the hell . . . Isn't there anything to this damn dress?"

"There are many women here tonight wearing much less." She lifted her chin and gazed past him into the room. "I was sick of wearing black. Now, don't you think we should find our table. Almost everyone is seated." She felt the fingers at her waist clench into her flesh and her body arched in response.

"I'll get you a Perrier first." Dev's voice was wooden as he led her toward the bar.

"I think I'll have a vodka martini, instead. Very dry."

"You never drink hard liquor." Dev's voice grated into her ear as he held her even closer to his body.

"Tonight I'm going to have a martini." Cle silently cursed the squeak in her voice, but the glide in her walk was smooth as she headed for the bar. She was dimly aware of the myriad eyes, both male and female, that followed her movements. She stopped in front of the small bar and put both hands on the cushioned edge, gripping it. The glittering smile she gave the man behind the bar brought him to her at once. "I'd like a vodka martini, please. Very dry."

"I'll just whisper the word vermouth as I pass you the glass. Is that dry enough, ma'am?" The bronze-haired young man grinned at her.

"Just right." Cle smiled back, feeling Dev behind her, his hand low on her spine. She watched the hand come round her and reach for the drink the bartender placed in front of her. Dev lifted the drink, her eyes following the motion of the glass until it reached his mouth. How she loved those firm lips, the lower one with a sensual fullness that softened whenever he looked at her!

"If you quaff this, my love, you'll be on your glorious derriere. Did you tell that besotted fool to make you a double?"

"Of course not, and he isn't a besotted fool. He was just being gracious," Cle snapped, holding out her hand as a demand for the drink. Dev gave it to her and she took a sip, trying not to shudder as the vodka slipped down her throat. She should have told the bartender to serve it on the rocks, then the melting ice could have lessened the kick of the raw liquor.

The bartender came back. "I made your martini with Balenkov's vodka, ma'am. That's the best we have and the strongest. One hundred and eighty proof! Just as strong as lemon extract, my wife tells me." The bartender moved back down the bar, laughing at his little joke.

"Wonderful," Cle whispered, blinking to keep her eyes from watering, aware that her vocal cords were being eroded and that her stomach was on fire. She felt the heat rise all the way to her face as she took another infinitesimal sip. Damn, she cursed herself. What a fool she was to have lived to this age without learning how to handle liquor.

She tried to smile up at Dev but her lips felt like rubber. "I'm ready to sit down now," she announced.

"You've never said a truer word." Dev ground his teeth, clamping onto her upper arm and leading her to one of the round tables in front of the raised dais and seating her. Oh, Lord, old Mr. Hopewell was sitting just above Cle where he would be watching her all through dinner. It was Cle's turn to grind her teeth as she thought of the interminable speech that the crusty old bear would make. Oh, sweet agony, there was his sister, Corinne, sitting on the other side of the stand where a microphone held center stage. As Dev drew his chair close, Cle took a gulp of the martini and started to cough.

"Will you cool down?" he hissed, patting her in an ungentle way on the back. "You'll be sick."

"I'll be dead if you don't stop beating me." Cle glowered at him, pulling her body away from him, then almost swaying out of the chair. She felt Dev's arm at once, pulling her back and heard him mutter, "Cle, behave."

Dev kept his arm around her for most of the dinner. And the dinner was a nightmare for her. The vodka had begun to make her queasy and the broiled lemon sole didn't help. When the dancing began she was feeling miserable, but she was also determined to hide it from Dev.

They had always danced well together, and she had always enjoyed it, but tonight was an endurance contest as she stumbled over his feet and kept mumbling her pardon.

When she saw a hand reach over Dev's shoulder to cut in, she turned with a sense of relief that she would be leaving Dev's company, that she wouldn't have to feel what she was sure was his censure.

As she turned, so did the room. It spun and dipped. "Oh, dear," a voice muttered sounding strangely like her own.

"What the bloody hell?" she heard Dev ask before the room darkened and fell away.

CHAPTER *Two*

CLE SURFACED IN PAIN, the whole world in blackness, and knew she had been in an automobile accident that had blinded her, broken every bone in her body, and fractured her skull. She probably had two hours to live. She shouted out Dev's name, wanting to tell him that the king-sized bed was now his, but all that came out was a croak. The croak jarred her whole body with pain.

"Want to go to the bathroom, darling?" Dev was laughing!

Maybe he was hysterical, Cle thought, trying not to move. "I'm blind, Dev."

"Blind drunk, I think. Here, let me take the cloth from your eyes. Lord, I haven't seen anyone so cold cocked by a double since I was at Harrow. You look awful, love. The bags under your eyes are blue, yellow, and pink." He looked satisfied.

"You're an unfeeling monster. I was probably poisoned by bathtub vodka and will die by slow, painful inches . . . ohhhhh" Cle gripped her head, then one hand clutched at her mouth. She jumped from the bed, aided by Dev who was chuckling.

He was still grinning when he lifted her head from the toilet bowl and wiped her mouth and face. "Now you're a perfect barberry green. The color clashes with your eyes. And as to your reference to bathtub vodka, I assure you, you can't blame this on anything but the *best* vodka. Stop reading so much F. Scott Fitzgerald. You just have a decidedly *classic* hangover!"

"I could have Asian flu." Cle moaned against his shoulder as he carried her back to bed. "You don't care what happens to me." A tear trickled down her cheek as she watched him tuck the blankets around her.

"I've told Toner you won't be in until tomorrow. I've left a note for Mrs. Hubbard to look in on you now and then, I'll be home early." Dev leaned over her, his hand pushing at her stringy hair, his lips brushing her clammy skin.

"What time is it, Dev? I should be up. There's so much to do for the fall collection. Jaime will be beside himself." Her voice was thready and she felt exhausted with the effort of speaking.

"Its eight-thirty in the morning and you are in no condition to go anywhere but to sleep." His face hardened, the strong bones pushing into the flesh of his face. "Damn Toner and his damned fall collection. I told him what I thought of his creation, too." Dev pivotted on his heel.

Cle wanted to argue with him but he strode out of the room so quickly, and besides there was the matter of her throbbing head, her paralyzed brain . . .

That evening when Dev returned home she was feeling better—and chastened. Cle had hurried Mrs. Hubbard out the door, assuring her that she could finish preparing dinner by herself. She wanted the time with Dev, alone.

She greeted him in the foyer, her hands clasped together, feeling the blood run up her neck when he paused to look at her before closing the front door.

A smile played around his mouth as his eyes roved her from head to foot, lingering on her face. "You look as though you might survive. I must say I like the color of your skin better this way than the green it was earlier. You're still a little pale."

"I still feel a little pale." Her smile was weak, her lips wobbling a bit. "Dev, I want to apologize for . . ."

"Is that the silk punjabi outfit I brought you from India last year? I love that blue and turquoise combination with your hair and eyes." Dev spoke softly, his hands reaching for her, the growl in his voice making the muscles in her stomach expand and contract like clenching fingers.

She responded to his kiss, welcoming his tongue, feeling the curl of heat grow in her lower body. She pushed at his shoulders wanting to finish what she had to say to him.

Dev allowed her lips to pull back a fraction.

"Dev, I didn't mean to embarrass you last evening. Was it very bad? I know how conservative the Hopewells are. Did they think . . . I mean, was it—"

"Hopey's sister Corinne sniffed a few times but the old boy was very understanding. He was worried more about you being sick, than about you being tipsy, love."

His hand swept down her spine in a soft caress. "You were more beautiful than any woman there. And, drunk or sober, you couldn't make me one bit ashamed of you." His strong white teeth nipped gently at her chin. "My opinion is the only one that matters in that firm, and they had better know and believe it." Dev's voice had the ruthless quality that crept into it from time to time. Cle had never been the brunt of it, but she was made fully aware that Dev was and had been for some time, master of his own destiny, kingpin of the firm and his family. He might not ever use his title, but there was a tinge of lèse majesté about him that could not be denied.

He lifted his head to look at her, the grin back in place. "Now are you going to feed me, or must I starve?"

Cle laughed, feeling somewhat more reassured than she had earlier. "I'm going to feed you . . . and it's a surprise." She urged him toward the stairs to go up and change, then rushed to the kitchen to see to the poaching of the salmon that had been flown in from the northernmost coast of Scotland. Dev had once told her that he thought the salmon caught off the coast of Scotland was the most succulent in the world. It had been Jaime who had put her in touch with an importer who had it flown in each day. Tonight seemed the golden time to serve it. Mrs. Hubbard had picked it up in the afternoon, then had fixed the rutabagas Dev said were a "must" to accompany the salmon poached in the driest and palest of sherries. The yellow turnip had never been a favorite with Cle because it was too smelly and strong. Baked in butter and lemon with coarse ground black pepper on the top, the vegetable had a mouth-watering appeal for her now. The salad was endive and hard-cooked egg with crumbled Roquefort, lightly coated with oil and vinegar.

Cle was stubborn about the wines they drank, insisting the upstate New York champagne, brut blanc de blanc, was the equal of French. She was a staunch New Yorker. She gave a last adjustment to the centerpiece of tiny pink roses and baby's breath and sighed deeply.

"Well, well, this is beautiful, darling. Are you going to seduce me?" Dev sauntered into the room, his long stride taking him to her side in an instant, his mouth a welcome pressure on hers. He reached around her into the ice bucket that stood next to his seat. "Ah, a very good year in New York, I know."

"Of course. There are no bad years in New York," Cle shot back, knowing he expected it.

He smiled down at her, his arm not releasing her as he lifted his head, a puzzled look crossing his face. "You know something smells just like Western Isle salmon. What is it?"

"Western Isle salmon!" Cle was gleeful as she watched his face change. Taking his hand she pulled him from the dining room into the kitchen proudly lifting the lid on the simmering liquid. Then she shooed him out to pour the wine while she made the final preparations and served. They ate with gusto, their enjoyment of the food and one another complete.

It was while they were having cheese and fruit that Cle broached the subject that had been gnawing at her. "Ah, Dev . . . What happened after I passed out? Was it awful for you?"

"I thought we talked that all out this morning," Dev said, pouring Drambuie into many-faceted crystal liqueur glasses.

"Well, yes, we did *some,* but you didn't say what happened at that moment." She squirmed in her chair, not looking at him. "Was I sprawled all over the floor? Oh, Lord, Dev, I've never acted like that."

He stood and came round to her, taking her hand to draw her to her feet, then leading her into the living room. When she protested that she wanted to clear things, he told her that they would do it together later. He pulled her down beside him on an overstuffed couch opposite its twin, also in the Wedgewood blue that was Cle's favorite color. "First of all, you didn't hit the floor. I caught you and before many people were aware of what happened I had taken you into an anteroom off the ballroom. Only Hopey was with me and he stayed just long enough to determine you weren't really ill. He made our excuses to guests and I brought you home." He leaned forward his mouth closing on her lower lip. "Stop chewing your lips that way. Only I can do that. Don't worry, I took you out of there through a cloakroom and down a back elevator to the underground garage."

"Oh, Dev, you didn't carry me all that way! I'm too heavy." Cle was anguished, squirming as he laughed.

"I think you were lighter when we first met. Now you're too contented. You're getting chubby."

"Pig!" Cle squawked, throwing herself atop him as he lay back on the cushions, pummeling him as his laughter increased.

They rolled off the couch, narrowly missing the tiny glasses of Drambuie as they continued to wrestle on the floor.

Cle was triumphant when she managed to pin Dev to the carpet. She clambered fully on top of him, stretching her arms on his to hold him in place. Then she looked down at him. "Gotcha."

"I surrender." Dev grinned up at her as his arms lifted hers in a slow backward movement. With no effort at all he freed his arms and clamped them around her. "Gotcha," he whispered, his one hand pulling her head down to his.

"That's not fair. You tricked me." Cle couldn't stop giggling while she struggled against Dev's hold.

"You know I'd do anything to hold you, angel," Dev drawled just before he fastened his mouth to hers and made her forget the hard glitter in his eyes when he spoke.

"Dev, don't you want to listen to music?" Cle mumbled, her arms tightening on his neck.

"Yes. You can sing to me while I make love to you," Dev muttered, frowning at the hook and eye fasteners on the punjabis. "Damn things! I'll rip them off you in another minute."

"Don't you dare, Devon Charles Albert Eldred Carstairs! I love this outfit." Cle glared at him, pushing him to one side so that she could undo the fasteners herself.

"Stop that," Dev said.

"Stop what?" Cle moaned, tugging the silk shirt from

the waistband of the matching pajama bottoms.

"Stop calling me by my full name. You know that annoys me. Besides, you forgot to include the name Willett before Charles. My family would never forgive you for such an omission."

"Your family would never forgive me anything." Cle gasped as his mouth sucked at her breast.

"It's not my family that you need to please. It's me," he drawled, drawing back to stare at her breasts with a deep, satisfied look on his face.

Though Cle could tell by the leaping green heat of his eyes that Dev was in the grip of the passion that always held both of them in thrall, she also knew that he would take his time looking at her as he always did. He made no secret of how he felt about her body. He gently tugged at the punjabi trousers, slowly drawing them down over her belly, thighs, knees . . . off completely. It was wildly erotic, as erotic as the way he began to stroke her from breast to thigh and back again. All the while he kept repeating, "Beautiful, beautiful."

It still amazed Cle at how unselfconscious she was with Dev, how delighted she felt that her body pleased him. And just as wonderful to her was how Dev's body seemed ever new and marvelous to her. She knew she wasn't an expert on men's bodies, but she was convinced that no man could have a more perfect body than Dev.

When the stroking hand took on a passionate tremor, Cle felt lost. Her own limbs seemed to be suffering from a bizarre heat that was melting them.

"You're mine," Dev growled in her ear, his body contracting spasmodically as she caressed him, the tactile delight his body gave her making her purr like a cat.

The mutterings of their love words increased as did the pace of their lovemaking. Then, deafened and blinded by their need for each other, their only awareness became the rhythm of their love. They moved in tandem, provoking and tantalizing one another, teasing and giving until they were frenzied and rushing to exquisite fulfillment.

Slowly, ever so slowly, they subsided. They lay entwined and Cle felt awash in a blissful, golden afterglow. Much later Dev lifted her and carried her to their bed.

Still held in his arms, Cle listened to the even tenor of his breathing as he slept beside her. Even his light snoring sounded like music to her and she snuggled closer to him. Dev. Even his name had charm, dignity, strength. He was all things good to her. She wanted all things good for him. Oh, they fought about some things. And Dev was certainly more possessive than she liked. That was surprising, Cle thought, lifting the hem of the silk sheet over Dev's shoulder. He hadn't appeared to be the possessive type when she first met him. On the contrary, his cynical attitude seemed to communicate a philosophy of taking pleasure where one could find it, going from woman to woman with the sure notion that variety could only be interesting.

Cle smiled to herself in the dark as she remembered the day they had met in the salon. Jaime himself had been waiting on Lady Clare Wellington and had insisted that Cle do some of the modeling, since Lady Clare's coloring was close to Cle's own deep black hair and porcelain complexion.

The obviously spoiled Lady Clare was with several friends who had always spent a great deal of money in Jaime's salon so the impromptu modeling of a few dresses turned into an almost complete show.

The giggling remarks about her bony figure that one of the women made would have embarrassed Cle had not Jaime been so supportive. But it wasn't until Dev walked into the salon and sat down with his cousin Clare and her friends, three women and a man, that Cle felt a hot nervousness.

Amy Worden, one of the black models, had hissed at her, gesturing her over to the curtain, then parting it just a fraction so that Cle could look out into the salon. To Cle's eyes Dev looked a bored, sophisticated, handsome man as she stared through the opening at him.

"Doesn't he look like Burt Reynolds, Cle?" Amy whispered, her mouth close to Cle's ear.

"He has more hair." Cle grinned at the other girl. "And smoother features."

"Oh, Cle, you're hopeless!" Amy moaned. "Smooth features! *Hair!* Why any fool knows that Burt Reynolds could be shaved from the top of his head to the tips of his toes and he'd still have it . . . that special 'yum-yum' only a few men have." Amy jerked her thumb at the curtain. "And that one out there has yum-yum and he'd have it if he had no hair at all. Do you get me?"

"Yes, I understand." Cle laughed at the other girl who was staring at her in a disgusted way. "But wait until you walk out on the runway and that 'Cecil darling' makes a funny remark just to make the ladies laugh, and you're the butt of the joke. You'll feel like dumping a cup of the fragrant tea they're drinking right on 'Cecil, darling's' head," Cle promised as her friend listened to Jaime's voice. Then Cle lifted her chin, assuming the modeling stance, and glided out to parade a strapless gown in white satin, reminiscent of the thirties. It had been the star attraction in Jaime's "Prohibition Collection." Jaime loved designing clothes typical of a particular era.

The next dress Cle had modeled looked deceptively simple. It was a cocktail dress, the hem just touching the knee, and composed of yards and yards of deep pink silk. The bodice was tight above a swirling skirt. A flesh-colored body stocking was worn under it and it looked perfectly respectable until Cle turned or moved in a fluid fashion. Then the skirt would flare out in puffs of silk revealing glimpses of what appeared to be Cle's nude body. It was provocative, expensive, and demanded a perfect figure to do it justice. Cle's body wasn't perfect.

She was too thin, but she was tall, her breasts were firm and rounded, and she moved like seeping oil in an unstudied motion that was part of her and totally untaught. Her legs were long and slender with delicate ankles that belied the years of swimming she had done in high school and college.

With the dress she wore black silk slings that cost more than her full month's salary. Her earrings were jet drops mounted in platinum, her hair had been twisted into a snake atop her head so that her slender neck and fine shoulder bones were delineated.

When she heard Jaime give the signal, she slid around the curtain and took the first stance.

Cle laughed to herself in the dark, still remembering the gasps of Lady Clare and her friends when she had twirled on the runway and "Cecil, darling" had gasped, "Good Lord, she's lovely!"

Dev had said nothing but when she had twirled again, nearer the seated people, she noticed that, though he was still lounging in his chair, there was an electricity emanating from him. Cle was made very aware that she had his unqualified attention.

She yawned and turned her face into his chest as she recalled how uncomfortable she began feeling after she had traveled the length of the runway twice. The mumblings and mutterings from Lady Clare and her friends were almost zero by the time Cle escaped through the curtain, but Dev's electric silence was a tangible thing.

Even though she knew that Jaime would be angry with her she cajoled Amy and another model, Suzanne, to finish the show for her. She escaped back to her cubbyhole and began working on the sketches she had devised to show to Jaime, sketches that he might choose to use for part of his spring collection that year. Instead of the flowing lines of skirts, dresses, or suits, a man's face had appeared under her pencil. When she realized it was the same man who had sat with Lady Clare and her friends, she had ripped the paper from the pad and crumpled it into the wastebasket.

She was still holding her head in her hands sometime later when Jaime came to her workroom.

"I should be very angry with you, Cleora. You know that I wanted you, not Suzanne, the finish to show." He lowered himself onto the corner of her tiny desk and reached a hand toward her worktable and drawing board. She thought he was about to pick up the sketches clipped to the top of the board when his supple fingers suddenly closed on her sketch pad.

When Cle made a grab for the pad, he held it easily out of her reach.

"What's this, my cool, cool Cleora? Drawing the clientele? Or just drawing the one?" Jaime's voice had an irritated twang to it. "Don't be too impressed by Lord Carstairs, Cle. Yes, I said Lord Carstairs, even though he has never used his title, it is still his. He is cousin to the charming Lady Clare Wellington and an international womanizer from what I hear," Jaime finished on a dry note. "With his money he can afford the 'best' of women, too."

Cle didn't attempt to plumb her own dejection at Jaime's words. "You sound as if you were envious, Jaime."

"Perhaps I am, a little." He shrugged, straightening from the desk and dropping the sketch he had torn from the pad into the wastebasket unaware of its counterpart all ready there. He leaned down to her, patting her cheek. "Still, I shouldn't complain. We sold five of the collection today including the Pink Moon cocktail dress you modeled." He turned to the door, then paused. "Bring those sketches to my studio tomorrow."

Cle had been elated but not even her swelling, optimistic feelings had obscured the picture in her mind of the darkly handsome Lord Carstairs who never used his title. He had a magnetic field that had drawn her to him as though she were a metal shaving.

She left the salon a little late that evening, knowing she would have to race for the bus that would take her across Manhattan to the Bronx. Her little apartment on the third floor of Mrs. Talasio's house was warm and cozy. The smells of southern Italian cooking rose from the kitchen into Cle's one room with bath and kitchenette.

She had been running head down through the cutting November wind, trying to avoid the deep pools of slush on the sidewalk, the aftermath of a sudden snow storm. She hadn't heard the car draw up to the curb next to her then cruise in front of her and stop, the passenger door opening. The "New York City caution" that had been hammered into her by stories told her by friends made her eye the car warily. She looked around to see if there was someone she could turn to for help just as the other door opened and Dev stepped from the car.

"Miss Orwell, I'm Devon Carstairs. I was in Toner's salon today with my cousin and her friends. I assure you I'm respectable and only want to give you a lift to your destination."

"I don't think... My bus will be coming." Cle had ducked her head and scooted past the car, breaking into the light jogging pace she used when she worked out. It was a little slippery but Cle kept going, praying that her bus would be as late as usual.

She was fighting her way through the cluster of people as her bus was pulling away from the curb. Desperation made her bang her gloved hand on the side of the bus but the driver never paused.

Cle took a deep breath and pushed her flyaway hair off her face. She felt shaken and a little out of breath. She gave a jerky step backward when the sleek Ferrari filled the space vacated by the bus.

"Get in, Miss Orwell, before you get spattered with

slush and I get arrested." The voice was less smooth, the harshness denoting irritation.

Cle giggled to herself in bed, letting her mouth touch Dev's chest. She had never figured out why at that certain moment she decided not to argue with him and get into the car.

The moment the door closed, shutting out the noise of Manhattan traffic in the early evening, she felt panic run with the blood in her veins, pacing the flow then increasing it. "I'm sure I'll take you out of your way . . . so if you can just manage to pass that bus right ahead of us, I can . . ."

"We'll have dinner, then I'll take you home, Miss Orwell. I want to talk to you."

"I'm not hungry. I'm in the habit of taking my main meal at noon. I eat very little in the evening." She cleared her throat trying to erase the squeak in her voice. "And I don't have much to talk with you about so if you don't mind . . ."

"I *do* mind." The voice had a velvet harshness that seemed menacing to Cle.

She shivered, edging toward the door.

"Miss Orwell, I have never raped a female in my life, nor have I ever so much as contemplated an assault."

"Get plenty of cooperation, do you?" Cle snapped, wanting to reach out for a handful of the November slush and dump it down the neck of his cashmere coat.

The hard laugh was accompanied by an assessing glance. "Beauty with a viper's tongue."

"Then I suggest you get rid of the viper's tongue and let me out right here." Cle had her hand on the car door.

"Forget it. It's locked electronically at the wheel. Now stop arguing with me." He swung the wheel in a ninety-degree turn down an alley, the car slewing a bit in the slush, then the tires took hold. He pulled into a parking place that led from the alley down under a building.

"I don't know where we are. I've never been here,"

Cle said, her eyes roving the darkened interior of the garage.

"I'm sure you haven't." Dev's grin had a lopsided twist to it as he helped her from the car and led her to an elevator.

"Don't get pompous with me, *Lord* Carstairs." Cle gasped as the hand at her elbow tightened into a numbing grip. "Stop that. It hurts."

"Then stop being so troublesome. I wasn't being pompous. This is a private club and I know most of the people who frequent it. I would have seen you or at least heard about you if you had been here." He turned her to face him as the elevator sped upward. "My name is Dev Carstairs. If you can't use my first name, call me mister, not lord. All right?" His voice was soft but the measured words left no doubt as to the rock-hard meaning.

"All right. I thought you were being condescending. I apologize if I was wrong." Cle looked at the wall of the elevator. She jumped as she felt his mouth on her cheek.

"You were wrong, darling. I would never patronize you."

Before Cle was on even keel, the elevator doors opened and the cacophony of voices and music precluded conversation.

The maître d' said something to Dev, then snapped his fingers to an underling who took their coats before he led them to a booth along the wall. The noise seemed appreciably less when they were cocooned in the leather privacy of the booth.

"Do you come here often?" Cle asked, feeling the hairs on her arm lift as he edged closer to her on the semicircular bench. "It certainly is lively."

Dev shrugged, the movement bringing his silk-coated arm in contact with hers. "Now and then. The food is good and if I feel like dancing, the music, too, is very good." He turned to look down into her face and Cle wanted to throw herself backwards. "Do you like to dance, Cle?"

"Ah . . . yes." She looked back at him, saliva filling her mouth. She wanted to swallow but her muscles were spastic.

"Good. We'll dance." He took one finger and ran it up her cheek into her hair. "I love your coloring, that blue-black hair with the china-white skin and sky-blue eyes. That could sound conceited, I suppose, since our coloring is similar." He lifted a strand of her hair to his mouth, his eyes never leaving her face.

"But your eyes are green," she murmured.

"Quite green," he said teasingly. Suddenly his expression turned serious. "After the fashion show, I asked Toner for your name. He didn't want to tell me but I was persistent. He's in love with you, isn't he? Do you feel the same about him?"

"What you're saying is ridiculous." Cle looked at him openmouthed. "Jaime is my boss and we have a very good working relationship . . . not that it's any of your business," she finished, her tone stiff.

Dev's smile spread that sensual mouth wide, live sparks seeming to leap from his eyes. "So Toner is just your boss, eh? Good. Any other boy friends?"

"Thousands. How about you? I'll want you to dump any old mistresses you might have hanging around and I trust your teeth are good. I should hate to have to pay for your braces." She smiled so wide she felt her jaw crack. "Of course, I'm assuming you don't have any debilitating disease. I can see you're no spring chicken."

"Very amusing. I'm thirty-six years old, in acceptable control of my faculties, and very, very attracted to you," Dev replied taking her hand and lifting one of her fingers into his mouth and chewing at it. "I've never wanted any woman so fast or so completely." He spoke in a surprised way, almost as though he were talking to himself.

"Big whip." Cle croaked, feeling her heart kick into high gear at his words. "I'm twenty-six and see so clearly that I can see right through you. I'm not at all attracted to you," she lied, struggling to keep her equilibrium with him.

They had ordered dinner but even now, lying in bed and concentrating on it, Cle did not remember what she ate or what she drank. She *did* remember dancing with Dev and feeling like a kamikaze pilot. No matter how she struggled, destiny was netting her in, tying her to Dev.

He had taken her home at two o'clock in the morning and they hardly spoke. He told her he would pick her up at Toner's right after work the next day.

Two weeks later she slept with him, delighting him because at her ripe old age of twenty-six she was still man-wary, inexperienced; and shocking herself because sleeping with Dev had seemed to be the most natural—and marvelous—thing in the world to do.

When she tried to explain her reticence at their first meeting she wound up explaining about Red Shafer the boy she had fully intended to marry. They attended the same college—he for engineering, she for art. By the beginning of their third year they had decided to marry after graduating and finding jobs. But in their senior year Red had been killed when he and some buddies had been coming home from a fraternity party at a nearby university. The car had skidded on icy pavement. "I dated other people of course but there was no one that I . . . well . . ." Cle stumbled, wondering with amused horror why she had opened herself up like that to Dev.

"Darling, I love you telling me all about yourself. Now I want to be your only man." He had kissed her ear. "You have a freshness about you, an inner beauty that I want for my own." His smile had a surprised possessiveness to it. "You've made me very happy by letting me love you, and from this moment on, I'm not going to lose you."

A week later she had moved to Dev's apartment, happy and confident that she was doing the right thing.

She relived those early months in her mind, relishing even the fights they'd had. Both she and Dev had independent natures and asserted themselves on every plane of life.

It was late when Cle's eyes fluttered shut, but there was a delightful contentment in her sleep, only lightly laced with an uneasiness that she couldn't fathom.

The next weeks were hectic for Cle and she sensed the increasing coldness in Dev as the time for his trip to Great Britain loomed close.

One evening as she dressed for a dinner they had promised to attend, she found herself nervous and all thumbs. She had put the thought of their separation into the deepest recesses of her mind but now in just days they would be parting for three weeks, maybe longer if Dev's work hit a snag.

Her hand shook as she tried to put on a sapphire teardrop earring. She dropped the screw-type back that acted as a fastener to the gold posts that held the sapphires. Cursing she fell to her knees, feeling around on the smooth surface of the Aubusson carpet. She knew they were antiques and even Dev's casual reference to them as mere trinkets he had picked up didn't lessen their value in Cle's eyes. If they had been glass from a wholesale junk dealer she would still have treasured them because they came from him.

"What the hell . . ." The low key anger in Dev's voice seemed to bounce off Cle's skin.

"I've dropped the sapphire earring back and you know it's the screw-type and not the ordinary push fastener," Cle babbled, not looking up from her search. In her peripheral vision she saw Dev's black silk-coated leg bend, showing the black silk of his socks as he came down next to her.

"Don't get too excited. They're just—"

"Don't you dare call them trinkets or I'll hit you," Cle's voice grated out, her eyes frantic as they combed the rug for the tiny gold screw.

"Ah, here it is, love. It was behind the leg of your dressing table stool. Here, let me do it for you." Dev smiled at her, holding the gold culprit in the palm of his hand.

Relief at having Dev smile at her after days of coolness and her own dejection over his departure brought the tears welling in Cle's eyes.

"Oh, Dev, I'm going to miss you when you go to London." Then she was in his arms, held tight to that strong chest.

"Then come with me. I want that so much. I want you to see my home, Larren. I want you to see my flat in Mayfair. Darling, there's so much I want to show you. Won't you come?"

"Dev, I can't. I told you . . ." She stopped speaking as she watched a now familiar shuttered look take away his smile. "Well, maybe, just maybe I could ask Jaime if I could pass this show and maybe he would let me do the spring one—"

Before Cle could finish she was clamped close to him, his mouth seeking hers. It was as though someone had released the flood gate. Dev's passion washed over her. In seconds she had forgotten the dinner, forgotten her earring, forgotten everything but Dev and that he wanted her with him.

He lifted his head, his strong mouth shaking. "Oh, darling talk to him right away, call him now. My God, you don't know how happy I'd feel if I thought you were coming with me."

"Me, too." She glowed. Her hands threading through his crisp black hair, the waves held in tight control, springing back in her fingers just as the grandfather clock boomed from the front foyer that it was seven o'clock.

Dev looked up, an irritated expression on his face. "We're late." He looked back down at her. "And I don't want to go at all." His eyes had that melted emerald look that always jammed Cle's pulse rate into overdrive.

"We promised. Clive Lawson is your best friend *and* he has to return to the embassy in Washington tomorrow," Cle said not even trying to hide the wistful note in her voice.

"Tough."

Cle laughed up at him as he let his fingers wander over her back. "You sounded like an American there for a moment."

"I feel like a man who could commit mayhem at the moment. I'm bloody sick of so many people deciding when we can be together. That has to change." Dev's eyes took on an opaque glint.

Cle lifted herself on her tiptoes to give him one last kiss before she turned to repair her lip gloss. "One of these days we'll run away to a desert island." Her voice lilted as she looked past her own image in the mirror to stare at Dev.

"Damn right." He let his hand slide down her back and gently cup her buttock. With a sigh then he stepped back and let her precede him out of the room.

In the warmth of Dev's Ferrari, their mute closeness was like electricity between them. Cle refused to let the doubts surface. How would she approach Jaime? Would he let her go? If she did go, how would Dev's family receive her? She might be an outsized sore thumb among the numerous Carstairs who would be called together to look her over. Then, would Dev see her as she really was—an ordinary upstate New Yorker who knew how to work hard and love harder?

When Dev led her up the wide fan-shaped steps leading to the double doors of the Georgian mansion, she looked around her, amazed at the contrasts on Long Island. On the forty-five-minute ride here, she had seen pockets of real poverty and neglect almost back to back with opulence. She paused for a moment under the stone portico and looked out over the grounds. "This is some weekend pad your friend Clive has."

Dev chuckled, his breath ruffling the hair at her temples. "Clive always had more money than he could handle. This place belonged to an American aunt of his. Naturally Clive inherited when she died. I say naturally because he is the only male member of his family, not that his three sisters suffer in any way. They don't. Come along, love." Dev smiled down at her as though he could feel her reluctance to meet his friends. Cle was always more relaxed with her friends rather than Dev's. With Dev, it was different. He was his smooth and sophisticated self with anyone.

Clive was on the heels of the butler who answered the door. "Devon, you dog, you're damn late. Ah, you have the beautiful Cleora with you. You'll have every woman here jealous, my lovely one. The ones that won't hate you for having that luscious body and face will hate you for having Devon Carstairs in tow. Come along, dear, I'll show you where the powder room is. Shall I?"

"No thank you. Just give me directions." Cle smiled her widest professional cheek stretcher.

Dev laughed, slapping his old friend on the back, the sudden glitter in his eyes a warning. "Cle is well aware of your wolfish ways, my friend. She doesn't like that type of treatment. I don't like it either." He turned to Cle. "I'll wait for you in the foyer, darling." His smile had a proud possessive tinge that had Cle reeling as she went to the powder room.

Dev was waiting at the bottom of the stairs when she started to descend, but now there was a group of people around him. Despite the speed with which she'd straightened her hair and checked her makeup, Dev had already collected a crowd. Cle felt a bitter taste in her mouth as she watched a chiffon-swathed creature fasten her hands to Dev's neck and attempt to pull his head down for a hello kiss.

"Will I have to wrestle them for you, darling?" Cle drawled, pausing on the stairs, letting her voice wrap like silk around the people below her. She was well aware of the theatrical effect she was having, being told by Jaime hundreds of times the value of stairs, the value of looking down on people in a queenly way. Cle used every trick in the book, letting her brows raise slowly, letting her eyes widen in surprise, then letting her mouth melt in a smile as her gaze rested on Dev.

His twist of a smile held complete comprehension. Not one whit of the irritation that he would be feeling was showing, but Cle knew only too well: he hated the artifice of modeling.

"Darling, you know the only one you have to wrestle is me." Dev's softly intimate tone made the others laugh. If some of the laughter had a brittle sound, no one would wonder, since most of the women there would have gladly traded places with Cle.

She continued her glide down the stairs right into Dev's outspread arms. She could feel his fingers digging into her.

"Very nice," he whispered. "Jaime would be proud of you but I would rather you didn't draw any more attention to yourself in front of these slavering fools. I would hate to have to break jaws at such a lovely function." Dev let his tongue just touch the edge of her ear, then he drew back, keeping one arm close around her.

The cocktail hour seemed to go on too long to Cle. As was her usual way, she was drinking Perrier and lime, the very notion of having any alcohol made her shudder as she thought of her last evening out with Dev. Booze was not for her.

The crowds of people shifted her away from Dev and

more than once she found herself fielding Clive's remarks. She took every chance to keep people other than him next to her and kept changing her position just to do that. At the same time she found herself farther and farther from Dev. At intervals she would see that strong head make a circuit of the room, then fix on her for a moment, the slight smile calling her back to his side.

It was during one of these dodging maneuvers, which she hoped would bring her closer to Dev, that she was edged into a small alcove. Before she could reenter the melee and get to Dev, she heard voices on the other side of a huge potted plant.

"She certainly can't hold him. No Carstairs would be caught dead married to a shop girl." The tones were sulfuric.

"Don't be an ass, Lydia. This isn't Victorian times and he isn't the Prince of Wales. Dev can marry whom he damn well chooses. And it seems to me, he's chosen Cle."

"He's stuck with her, you mean. Oh, it's all right in this country, but can you see her taking her place at Larren! God, even the horses wouldn't accept her, Clive. You know what it's like there. The people will despise her."

"That's balderdash and you know it, my dear. Some of our loftiest peers have married out of their class *and* they are happy."

"Dev is different. Clare told me that under all that kidding he does about the peerage, he takes his family obligations very seriously. If ever he was forced to marry her, he would end up being very bitter. No doubt he would even end up divorcing her, just so that he could marry someone of his own kind."

"My dear Lydia, that's twaddle. Your trouble is that you're jealous. . . ."

"Jealous? Me? Damn you, Clive—"

Cle didn't wait to hear any more. She felt as though

she had just stepped through hot glass. She could feel the burning cuts all over her body as she walked with a fixed stare toward the stairs and the powder room.

She was sure she heard her name, that she heard Dev's voice but she kept the sleepwalker's pace toward the nebulous sanctuary of the ladies room. God, all the ghostly doubts that she had buried in her mind flared into painful life. Dev couldn't be hers . . .

CHAPTER *Three*

CLE STOOD THERE SHAKING, her hands clenching and unclenching at her side, the slamming of the door reverberating through the apartment. Dev was gone. The loud, angry confrontations between them for the last three days seemed to echo through the now-silent apartment. Dev was gone. He was gone to England and she was here.

For the past three days, Dev had ranted and raved at her, trying to make her tell him why she had changed her mind about accompanying him to England. No matter what reason she gave him he shouted her down, saying that he didn't believe her and asking why she was doing this.

"Damn you to hell, Cle," he had snarled at her. "What are you keeping from me? Why didn't you ask Toner... No, dammit why didn't you *tell* Toner you were going? Better yet I would have told him. What game are you playing? I won't have it."

"I told you I'm not going with you. You can't make me go."

"Damn you, I'll tie you in a bag and drag you on that plane." There was murder in his green eyes.

Cle had watched him openmouthed just before he left. She saw the smooth, sophisticated lawyer, the polished solicitor peeled away, stripped to the raw menacing man who looked at her as though he wanted to flay her. That was his last look at her before he flung himself out the door.

She readied herself for work three times. She ran her pantyhose, smeared her lip gloss, pulled a button from her blouse. When she finally looked at the finished product in the mirror, she saw a wraith with banjo eyes, the circles beneath almost the same blue. Her skin was paper white and not even blusher disguised the parchment look. The five pounds that had melted from her frame in the last three days made her skirt swivel at her waist.

When she reached the salon, she went right to her little cubicle, planning to tell Jaime that she would miss the regular conference because she was too busy with the line.

Jaime forestalled this by coming down to her. When he shut the door, closing the two of them into the cell-like room, Cle took a deep breath. "You might well sigh. You were thirty minutes late today. I called you every five minutes before phoning the doorman and telling him to buzz me when Her Highness made her entrance. What the hell is wrong with you? Are you sick?" Jaime wrenched her chin around, leaning over her as she sat at her drawing board. "Tell me, Cle. What happened? Are you under the weather?" Jaime's narrowed eyes widened in comprehension. "It's his lordship, isn't it? Has he skipped out on you?"

For a moment Cle wasn't going to answer. She hugged

her misery to her like a winter coat in a snow storm. Then she felt too full to hold any more and it spilled from her mouth. "In a way you could say that. He's gone to England. I didn't go with him."

"Good. It wouldn't have been right for you, Cle. His kind aren't for you. This is where you belong. We're your people."

"I love him Jaime. That's my problem. I think that's been my problem from the start. Oh, I know I loved him right away but I thought it was a modern easy love that I could walk away from with a sad smile and a lot of good memories. I can't. I'm cut to pieces." Cle could feel the smile on her face slip sideways. Shudders crashed through her body like incoming tide on a shore. "I never once thought he would become my whole life. The laugh is on me." The tight dryness of her voice was echoed in her eyes.

"God, Cle, don't! Cry. Do something. I can't bear to see you like this." Jaime's voice had a surprised hurt to it.

"Don't look like that Jaime. I'll be fine. Just don't ask me to come to the conference today."

Jaime had nodded and left her, his face troubled.

In the ensuing days, it seemed to Cle that Jaime hovered close but she barely took note of his presence. She poured every bit of energy she had into the new collection.

She hadn't expected to hear from Dev the first days after his departure, but she had hoped. When a week passed and she hadn't heard from him, she was convinced that he didn't want her around any more.

One day when she was in Jaime's studio, Dev seemed to loom in her mind. She couldn't concentrate.

Finally Jaime slammed down the pointer he was using and threw her a disgusted look. "All right, Cle. You have to get over this. You're no good to yourself or to me. You need to get away for a few days."

"I need to get away for a long time," she burst out, her voice raw, bitter. "I'd like to disappear."

Jaime's mouth opened then shut again. He put his right hand up to his chin, rubbing in slow motion. "Would you now? Get away is that it? That might be arranged, Cle, and it would be a help to me as well as you." He walked over to her and lifted her from the chair. "Go back to your board. I have a few calls to make. I'll come down to you in a little while."

Cle tried to work in Jaime's absence but her mind felt like a sodden sponge. It could hold no more.

She was still doodling on her sketch pad thirty minutes later when Jaime stepped into her cubicle, closed the door, and looked at her with gremlin glee. He opened a brown paper bag and removed a jar of peanut butter and some English crackers and one solid silver knife, gleaming rich in the fluorescent light.

"We celebrate, my dove. I've just talked to Max Brainerd and he tells me he is still interested in having a protégé of mine come out and give him some ideas. He was very enthusiastic when I mentioned your name because he and I had talked of you in our last conversation. He would love you to come. What do you say, Cle? Would you like to work for Brainerd for a year or two, then come back to me?"

"Australia!" Cle looked at him, mouth agape. "I never thought of going so far away."

"It would help you at this point in your life. Then you could always come back to me when you'd gotten over Carstairs."

Cle's eyes flashed to his face, pain like lava flowing through her veins.

Jaime touched her cheek with one finger. "Yes, you'll get over him, little Cleora, then you and I will work together again. That's the way it should be. Not this way, you wasting away, pining like one of those old-time heroines. He isn't worth it. You don't fit in his life and you don't want to. This is the life for you. Am I right?"

"I'll . . . I'll think about it, Jaime. I'll tell you tomorrow what I've decided."

Jaime had frowned but then shrugged.

All the way home Cle prayed that Dev would call. She had never imagined that being parted from him could cause this much pain. She felt as though someone had amputated her arms without anesthesia. The blood dripped from her body and there was no staunching the wounds. She had to have a phone call from him to save her life.

She paced the apartment the whole evening, waiting for the phone to ring just as she had on all the other evenings since Dev's departure. Only tonight the feeling of loss was more intense. Tonight she would make the decision to stay or leave him forever.

At dawn she was lying staring at the ceiling. Dev was so angry when he left. He hadn't tried to make it up. She felt certain he was through with her. Pain had turned into numbness. She had to get out of his apartment. She would leave a note for Mrs. Hubbard telling her that she would be leaving for a while. By the time Dev returned to America in two weeks' time, she would be in Australia, starting a new life.

The following days were awful, but Jaime managed to smooth the rough edges for her. He had insisted that Amy Worden accompany Cle to get her passport and her shots. He swore it was because he didn't want her to shame him that he had given her such a fine collection of clothes for her very own.

Cle tried to protest, but she was so cocooned in misery her words seemed to have no impact. Amy's sympathy was overt and would have embarrassed Cle had she the strength to feel such an emotion.

It seemed to her that an automaton, not her own self, packed her luggage and directed Mrs. Hubbard to send the other things to storage. When the woman asked her about her whereabouts, Cle directed her to send all mail and queries to Toner. She could tell the older woman was displeased by the lack of information, but Cle was determined to cut herself off from all ties to New York until she did, in Jaime's words, "get over Dev." She didn't probe too deeply into the despair that rolled over her at such a thought. She gritted her teeth, willing her thoughts, ahead of her body, to Sydney, Australia, land of sunshine, beauty, and forgetfulness.

She had no memory of getting on the plane after her watery farewells with Amy. Jaime had a grim-faced look when he kissed her good-bye, surprising Cle by kissing her on the lips.

All her life she had wanted to go to Hawaii. She and Dev had talked of taking a trip to the enchanted islands one day. It was an effort to smile when a young man draped a lei about her neck. She felt a stirring of interest when she looked at Diamond Head against the skyline but she wasn't unhappy that she only had an hour layover. She took little interest after that, deciding to force herself to work so that she would be ready with some new sketches to show Max Brainerd.

They landed at Sydney in the early evening. Cle was unprepared for the daylight, expecting darkness and coolness. She had forgotten that in Sydney it would be like late spring back home, that the approaching Christmas season signaled days on the beach to Australians not days on the ski slopes as it would to a New Yorker.

Max Brainerd met her himself, surprising her. She studied the medium build, sandy haired man in front of her and thought how much like Jaime he looked. She felt the first real smile on her face for days.

Max cocked his head, his bushy eyebrows café au

lait-colored and mobile. "I know. People used to think we were brothers when we studied together in Paris. Of course I'm much more talented than Jaime, but he's quite good."

Cle laughed.

"Come, my dear, I have a lovely flat for you not too far from the salon. It's the top floor of an old warehouse on a street of lovely little shops. The second floor is the storage area. The third floor is your flat. There is a private elevator that leads from the street and it's quite spacious. A friend of mine owns the building and renovated the top floor for his own use but now his work takes him to London for . . . whatever is wrong, my dear. You've gone white on me. Are you ill? Jet lag?"

"Nothing really. Maybe a bit of jet lag." Cle smiled weakly, wondering if the word London would ever stop lacerating her.

Cle was glad for the spectacular view as they drove into the city. "Are all sundowns so splendid?" she whispered to Max, afraid to break the kaleidoscope spell cast by the lowering sun.

"Just for tourists, my dear." Max chuckled.

Cle was so busy rubbernecking that she didn't even notice the direction they took. For her the trip was all too fast. The wonderful city bathed in orchid twilight seemed to have the look of the enchanted land of Oz. Cle had a sudden curl of hope inside.

She was delighted with the apartment. It was spacious and had a rough-hewn elegance that was both masculine and tasteful. It was nothing like the sophisticated decor of Dev's apartment. Much of the wall space was covered by honey-colored paneling. The drapes were swagged back sheers in gold and barely covered the panoramic glass windows that looked out over a park-like area. She turned back to a smiling Max. "It's lovely and so homey. I never expected a park."

"Sydney is one big park. It's a beautiful city and I think you'll be happy here. Is there anything I can do to get you settled?"

Cle shook her head, smiling, all at once wanting to curl into a bed and sleep. Sleep! She hadn't slept in so long but tonight she was sure she was going to do just that. "I'll be fine. I'll just unpack an overnight bag for now."

Max nodded his head. "I'm glad you're here, Cle. Jaime praised you to the skies. I'm surprised he allowed you to come he's so fond of you."

Cle let go an inaudible sigh. Jaime hadn't told him about Dev. She was grateful. "Jaime is a good friend and a wonderful teacher. I just hope that I can be of some use to you."

"Oh, I think you can. I'm anxious to see your sketches." He paused for a moment, a slight frown on his face. "Would you like to take tomorrow off and begin the next day?"

"No. I'd like to get started right away. If you could give me directions to the salon . . ."

"I shall pick you up myself. Say, eight-thirty?"

After Max left she roamed the apartment, liking it more and more. She was delighted with the luxury of two bedrooms. She would be able to use one as a work-room. She walked from there back into the room Max called the lounge. It was a huge square room that had a large dining alcove two steps up from one side, and long angled windows all along the side that had the effect of skylights. The random width floors had rich looking Chinese carpets on them in jewel tones of blue and pearl that were a wild but pleasing contrast to the honey paneling. There was a stone fireplace with twin overstuffed couches in blue nubby cloth facing each other over a round honey-colored wood table.

She wandered from there to the very modern kitchen where again the honey-colored paneling was repeated.

Cle sighed with satisfaction and ambled to the bathroom that opened off the master bedroom. She liked the brown and cream marble decor of the bath and sunk into the salted depths of the tub to wash the grime and aches from her body. For one stark moment she had a wish for an inner massage that would take away the pain of wanting Dev.

For the first time in many days she hit the pillow and slept at the same time. She didn't waken until a persistent sound in her ear disturbed her. She blinked at the strange surroundings trying to orient herself. It was a few moments before she realized that the phone was ringing next to the bed. "Yes?"

The laughter was friendly. "It's Max, Cle. It's seven o'clock. Let me pick you up early and we'll have breakfast. Is that all right with you?"

"Oh . . . ah. That sounds good. Give me twenty minutes and I'll meet you at the door." Cle tried to stifle a yawn, blinking her eyes to keep them open.

"Fine. I'll be standing next to the elevator timing you."

Cle could hear Max's laughter as she dropped the phone onto its cradle and streaked for the bathroom, filling her arms with hose and lingerie along the way. She promised herself that she would unpack fully that evening, frowning at the open suitcase with its trailing contents.

The elevator doors opened as her watch told her she had one minute to spare.

A lounging Max Brainerd looked at her openmouthed. "A punctual woman! God, I thought they were extinct."

"Very funny." She gave him a haughty glare. "I'll have you know that I have less trouble with women being tardy than I do men."

"Bushwaugh, my dear. My clients—all females, mind—are invariably late," Max said, his voice a bit pompous.

"And I'll bet that you still keep them waiting," Cle shot at him, willing to wager he had the same attitude as Jaime.

Max's hesitation made Cle snort in satisfaction.

"My dear, would you have me, the great Max Brainerd, cool my heels for a pack of brainless women?" He'd escorted her to his car and held open the passenger door for her.

She held his eye. "Is that why they pick your salon, because they're stupid?" She slid into the car.

"In that way they're smart." Max gave an exaggerated sigh before going round to slip beneath the wheel. "Why didn't my friend Jaime tell me that you had a biting tongue?"

Cle laughed then looked straight ahead, through the windshield as they pulled into the traffic. "I had a friend who once said that . . ." Cle caught herself in horror realizing she was going to repeat something Dev had said to her about being "beauty with a viper's tongue."

"What is it, Cle? You've turned pasty white. Are you ill? What were you saying about your friend?" Max fired the questions like missiles, his head going from Cle to watching the traffic in a rapid swiveling motion.

"I'm not ill. I was just going to say that this person thought I had a quick tongue, too." She looked out the window on her side hardly seeing the people bustling to work. Dev. Would she never get him out of her mind?

She made a big effort to listen and respond to Max as he led her into a café-type restaurant and proceeded to order for her an American breakfast of eggs, sausage, and toast and oatmeal and kippers for himself. Cle was delighted when they were served a delicious coffee instead of the tea she had expected.

"I would have eaten the kippers and oatmeal, you know," she said, smiling.

"I was just thinking how nice eggs and sausage sounded." Max made a face at her when she laughed.

"Jaime said that you have some fabulous silks that you use. Do you get them from Japan?" Cle sipped her coffee with relish, finding it strong and delicious.

"No. Japan is too expensive. We have a silk industry here in Australia and we get some of our silks from the less industrialized countries in Asia. As you no doubt know, our country has all the climes, from cold to tropical, so we use the woolens too for which we are very famous, but we also can grow the mulberry tree with some success so the silkworm is made quite happy." Max waxed enthusiastic when he discussed the fabrics of his country and, when he realized that Cle was deeply interested, his talk became more detailed.

Both Max and Cle were shocked when they noticed that it was almost eight-thirty. They hurried to the salon. Her introduction to the staff at Max's, for that was the name of his establishment, was eased by Max himself, who introduced her to his personal staff. Then he left her in the capable hands of Alistair Nivens who showed her the workrooms, the vault, and introduced her to the modistes and the mannequins.

The days sped by and to Cle's relief there were long periods when Dev's face was not in front of her.

The friendly Australians made her first weeks not only pleasant but interesting. As Christmas approached, she had many invitations to dinner and to beach parties. Alistair Nivens had a beach house and it was decided that Max and Cle would spend the two-day holiday with him and his wife and a few friends.

One evening in her apartment she was poring over some sketches when the phone rang. She jumped, staring at it from her place on the couch. She lifted the receiver on the fourth ring and heard the operator inquire if she were Cle Orwell. "Jaime? Jaime, is that you? Lord, why did you call person to person? It must be costing a mint."

"Yes, it is costing, darling, but I wanted to make sure

that I reached *you!*" Jaime launched into a monologue, full of anecdotes about happenings at the salon. It was as though he were calling from the corner drugstore.

Cle could feel the tension of the last weeks break away in chunks as Jaime described how Amy had stuck out her tongue at a customer who had made the incautious remark about Amy being rather good looking for a black girl.

"I damn near lost a million-dollar account but I couldn't be angry at Amy. I would have done it myself if I had heard it."

"Oh, Jaime, it's so good to hear your voice. Please give my love to Amy and Suzy and the staff."

"I will, dear." There was a long pause. "Cle, Carstairs has been here *maxi* times and he has murder in his eyes."

Cle's limbs felt as though they were melting wax. Lucky Jaime! He had seen Dev. Poor Jaime! Dev could be the very devil when fury rode him. "I . . . I hope he isn't making you too uncomfortable, Jaime."

"Darling, he wants to kill me, and I think he would except that he considers me his only link to you." There was irritated awe in Jaime's voice. "I never thought I would see that arctic facade of his lordship crack . . . but, dammit, I sure have. He wants you back, Cle. That I know."

"I'm sure of it." Cle could feel her smile tipping to one side. "Dev would never allow himself to be dumped. *He* can dump, but no one can do it to him. He must be livid."

"Sulfurous, darling. Smoke curls out of his ears and nose. I never believed in the Nether World until I watched 'is Ludship inquire about you. If I didn't know the breed better, I would say he was desperate." Jaime coughed once. "But don't worry, darling, he has gotten nothing from me nor will he. Now for some good news. I have decided to take a little time off from the slush and cold and fly to Australia to visit you and Max. Oh, not to fear I will let the cat out of the bag to Carstairs. I had my travel agent book me through from International Airport in Toronto. If anyone checks, I've gone north into ski country. Good, huh?"

"Very good." Cle's voice was hoarse.

"I should be there sometime between Christmas and New Year's day. I'm not just sure which day but I'll call you from one of our layovers. Ta, Cle. I think I'll deduct the charge for this call from your first salary check when you return."

"That's what you think, you—" Cle broke off and laughed as she realized she was talking to the burr of a line gone dead. Jaime had ended their conversation with the dramatic flourish he affected in his work. Cle's hand shook as she replaced the phone.

Oh, Dev, won't you ever leave me alone? she cried silently. I *will* live without you! *I will!* She grated her teeth, cursing the weakness in her that kept the picture of him so clear in her mind.

Christmas came to Sydney with sunshine and picnics and promises that she would learn how to handle a surfboard in no time. Cle was skeptical as she listened to Max describe the learning of the skill that seemed so natural to Australians, Hawaiians, and Californians. She couldn't forget she was a New Yorker. The drive to Alistair's beach house was not a long one but it gave Cle a chance to see the sun-drenched beaches that seemed to stretch to infinity.

Max glanced over his shoulder to see if he could pass a car and grimaced. "Cle, did you have to bring so many gifts? Lord, did you bring two for everyone? I want you to know that I wasn't fond of all that wrapping either." He frowned at her.

"You know you loved it." Cle smiled at the man who

had become a friend to her in such a short time. "You shook your own gift for ten minutes trying to figure out what it was."

"I just hope you paid a fortune for it. I'm worth every penny." Max gave her a pleased look when she laughed.

Alistair's beach house was a rough wood affair that overlooked craggy rocks that seemed as though they'd been thrown there by a giant hand. Beyond the rocks was whitish sand with darker, volcanic sand rimming the water. Monstrous waves crashed onto the shore.

Cle inhaled the tangy salt air and felt a tinge of excitement. Alistair's wife, Diana, was an artist and, as she stood next to Cle, she smiled at her.

"Magnificent, isn't it? I see it every morning and every day it's new and different."

"Aren't you afraid of sharks when you surf?" Cle asked raising her voice to be heard over the roar of the waves.

"We have some of the largest sharks in the world off the coast of Australia and anyone who isn't wary of them is a fool, but I can't say that we have ever had much trouble with them here and we've lived here for eight years."

Over lunch Cle discovered how delightful the company was. Everyone was friendly and eager to show her all the rudiments of surfing. Later, when she appeared in a one-piece lycra bathing suit, she felt Max's eyes on her.

"No wonder, Jaime is so protective of you, Cle. You are quite lovely." He looked at the slight frown on her face and shrugged, lifting her board to his shoulder and carrying it to the water's edge.

Cle felt awkward and nervous when she tried to grasp the board as the others were doing. All at once she had the feeling that she should announce it was too soon after lunch to swim or that the waves looked too dangerous, or . . .

"Feeling edgy, Cle? Everyone does the first time but you'll like it once you try it. It takes years and dedication to be expert at this sport but even a novice can have fun if she's careful. Come along now, push your board out and lie on it full length. I'll be right next to you."

Cle could feel her heart pounding as she paddled out over those deep troughs. Neither she nor Max paddled out as far as the others, Cle turning her board as Max directed then looking over her shoulder at the rollers that seemed to come endlessly.

"Here comes a nice one for us, Cle. It's small."

Cle gulped, thinking Max must be out of his mind if he called that crusher galloping up behind them *small*. She did as he said, though, and began paddling toward the beach and when she felt the upward thrust of the wave she pulled her legs up under her until she was kneeling. She couldn't bring herself to stand as Max was doing, but still she got an enormous thrill from the ride. She tumbled from the board as it slid into shore. Laughing and shaking out her hair, she called to Max. "That was fabulous. Let's do it again."

Cle felt all her muscles come into play as she tried the board again and again, sometimes simply losing balance and falling down, several times being plowed down by the force of the water. It was exhilarating, it was dangerous, and she welcomed the deep fatigue that affected her when they called a halt.

"Dear Lord, Cle," the woman named Pam exclaimed, "you're in better shape than all of us. If I had done this much on my first time out I would have been stiff for a month."

Cle gave her a rueful smile. "I'll be stiff, I'm sure, but it's worth it. I loved it. No wonder you Australians are always smiling. You work off all your tensions in that lovely surf."

The others laughed and made teasing remarks to one another about her observation. She felt very much at home. Then, too, the knowledge that she was so tired that she would undoubtedly sleep through this Christmas Eve night made her glad. She was afraid of more torture from memories of how Dev had awakened her every hour last year to cuddle and love her and each time had given her a small, beautifully-wrapped gift. She could still see Dev's elfin grin when she chided him for his extravagance in buying her so many things and how he'd kissed her. Then he'd told her not to lecture him, that he had sent a check in an amount equal to all the gifts he'd bought to Mother Theresa of Calcutta—and in her name. Cle had cried and hugged him hard. She'd mumbled over and over, "I love you, I love you," but perhaps not loud enough for Dev to hear.

She was glad when dinner that evening was loud and raucous. She was grateful for Alistair's two children, who were so excited they could hardly eat. It felt good to watch the children tear into the two gifts they were allowed to open on Christmas Eve and sing the Christmas carols. She hoped the others would take the mistiness in her eyes for sentimentality.

"It's hard to be away from your own country and people on Christmas, but soon, Cle, you will think of us as your people."

Cle gave Max a grateful smile and allowed him to kiss her under the mistletoe.

Jaime called from Hawaii two days before New Year's Eve to tell her that he would be there to celebrate with her and Max. They met Jaime's plane and it seemed that they were all talking at once. He was going to stay with Max during his visit and he seemed especially pleased that Cle had decided to give a small party in his honor on New Year's Eve.

"I'm anxious to see this place you have raved so much about, dear Cle." Jaime squeezed her shoulder as she sat between the two men on the front seat of the car.

"I didn't rave. After all I've only talked to you once and written to you twice."

"Well, it sounded like raving." Jaime shrugged, smiling at her.

For the rest of the journey to Max's apartment, Cle was content to listen to the two experts argue the merits of the business that engrossed them.

Cle was delighted by the small catering firm Max had recommended—and relieved to discover Max was correct in saying they were not expensive. Unlike Jaime who had an imperial notion of what was "frugal," Max was realistic. The caterer was well within Cle's budget and so on New Year's Eve day she found herself, with Max's blessing, taking the day off to do the last-minute cleaning that she thought was necessary. She was horrified at Jaime's offer to help, knowing that he would sit around, drink gallons of coffee, and distract her with talk about the world of high fashion. She was grateful when Max coaxed him into visiting a weaver that he considered a master.

Hair tied in a kerchief, Cle waxed the wood paneling in the lounge and dining room. She had worked her way into the kitchen feeling very satisfied with the two rooms she had finished, when the doorbell started ringing. Someone was leaning on the bell and, thinking it was an overburdened caterer, Cle flung the door open.

"Happy New Year, Cle!" Dev leaned against the door jamb, his indolent pose belied by the green sulfur of his eyes. "Aren't you going to invite me in?"

CHAPTER

Four

OPENMOUTHED, CLE STARED, not really able to believe that Dev was actually standing in front of her. The stun of surprise wore off within seconds, though, and she tried to shut the door on him.

Dev slowly forced the door wide, shoving a straining Cle behind it. "Not very friendly of you, darling, and after all we've meant to each other." His voice sounded like a fingernail down a blackboard.

She had to grit her teeth to keep from screaming. Inhaling deeply, she faced him in the paneled foyer. "Get out of here. What are you doing here? You can't stay."

"I can see you're overcome with joy at my presence, so much so that your speech is erratic. You're talking like a robot whose batteries have run down, love," Dev drawled, unbuttoning his sport coat as casually as if he'd just come home from work and nothing was wrong between them. He ambled past her toward the lounge area, his eyes moving in narrow assessment over the apartment.

"How like you to make some remark about my speech, m'lud," Cle grated, yanking the kerchief from her head and following him, stopping dead on the top step leading down into the living room when Dev whirled on her, his face a savage mask.

"Don't get nasty, Cle. I can get a great deal nastier and have bloody better reasons." His voice had the sound of a sledgehammer hitting concrete. His eyes were just as Jaime had described them. Green sulfur . . . and murderous!

Cle licked her lips, thrusting out her chin. "What are you doing here?"

"Now what the bloody hell do you think I'm doing here?"

"I realize you're angry with me, but . . . but I did what I thought was . . ." Cle's voice trailed off as she watched his features contort.

"Yes. You had better stop talking, Cle. I don't know how far my control will stretch, but I would guess not far." Dev's head swiveled until his eyes lighted on the decanter and glasses sitting on a small table next to the fireplace. He strode across the room in four thrusting moves. His hand tilted a large measure of sherry into a glass. He tossed off the first then upended another into his mouth. He stood there staring at the decanter in his hand for long moments before he looked at her again. "Do we talk now or at some later date?"

Cle's instinct was to run and hide in a closet and stay there for a year. She had to force the words from her throat. "I . . . I'm having guests this evening. It's New Year's Eve . . ."

"I'm aware of the day and time." His voice was silkily sarcastic and made Cle shiver. "I'm sure you'll want to be polite and issue me an invitation as well."

"Oh, I will, will I? Think again, Dev." She stared at him. "How long are you going to be in Sydney?" she croaked.

"As long as it takes."

He was all steel heavily wrapped in velvet—terribly threatening and Cle felt shaky. "You're talking in riddles."

"If you want straight answers, ask straight questions." His eyes swung away from the Chinese rug and fell full on her. "While I'm here, I'll want to see Sydney. You can show it to me."

"I'm not a tour guide." Cle watched his lips peel back from his teeth at her words and took a step backward. She cleared her throat. "I still have work to finish before my guests arrive . . . so . . . if you don't mind."

He glowered at her. "Why haven't you hired a daily to take care of the work? It's nonsense for you to be doing all this manual labor and then expect to entertain this evening."

Cle's chin came up, her hands pulling the kerchief between them like a rope. "I don't have unlimited funds. And don't make some snide remark about that, please! Besides, I enjoy doing some of the housework, even though I can't do it all." She braced herself, remembering Dev's irritation with her when she would insist on doing some of the household tasks herself rather than save them for Mrs. Hubbard.

He stared at her for long moments. "All right. We'll do it together."

Cle felt her mouth drop, her eyes start from her head. "Don't be silly," she whispered, her voice hoarse.

"Don't be pompous, Cle. It's unattractive." Dev pointed to her apron. "Get me one of those wraparound things."

"But you can't . . . Your slacks . . ." Cle paused, his words sinking in. Anger seemed to rise from her toes. *"Pompous!"* she shouted at him as she followed him at a trot to the kitchen. "Did you say pompous?" She stood in the doorway leading to the pantry where Dev was rummaging around. "You have gall, I'll give you that. How dare you say that I—"

"Don't nag me," Dev said as he emerged from the pantry with the vacuum cleaner in one hand, pail with cloths and cleaners in the other, apron round his waist. "If you want this place done, get working. I'll argue with you later."

Cle could feel her blood pounding in her head. Every epithet that she could dredge up was clamoring to be shouted at Dev as he walked past her into the living room, ignoring her. Frustration drove her after him but since he continued to pretend she wasn't there and then turned the vacuum on so that her voice disappeared in the roar, she had no choice but to go back to her polishing.

Anger made the cloth a live thing and in no time Cle finished her waxing. She and Dev barely exchanged a word. The place looked wonderful when they called a halt some hours later. Grudgingly she offered Dev a sandwich and something to drink and still there were few words between them.

Cle was still groping for some way to make it clear to Dev that he should not show up that evening when he abruptly rose to his feet, said that he was going, and that he would be back later.

She was left staring at the door he slammed behind him and listening to the hum of the elevator that took him to the ground floor.

Cle soaked in a hot tub with mountains of fragrant bubbles, hoping to calm her nerves. From time to time she eyed the dress she had hung on the clothes tree in the bedroom. Swathed in a bathsheet, she walked around the dress several times trying to decide if, in truth, Jaime's creation would give her courage, as he had told her it would when he first insisted that she have it. She'd shot back that she'd probably be arrested for wearing what he termed his "Venus Creation."

It was a strapless cream lace dress worn with a sheer body stocking underneath. It was form hugging, hidden pleats from the knee providing the freedom to dance . . . or walk! It delineated every curve, leaving very little to the imagination.

Cle creamed her body with a perfumed lotion given to her by Amy Worden who said, "it was guaranteed to gather the 'yum-yum' boys to her side." She had scoffed but now, as she inhaled the elusive scent that emanated from her body, she raised her eyebrows. She was glad the apartment was air conditioned as she dabbed at the beading of perspiration on her lip but decided not to turn the power to high until the press of people would demand it. She used very little makeup, grateful that her skin had already picked up a honey tan from the day of surfing at the Nivens's. A touch of blush, a light eye makeup, lipstick and she was finished.

Remembering Jaime's admonition against too much jewelry, she wore only the teardrop sapphires Dev had given her and a pinkie ring with a tiny sapphire stone. Her hair fell straight to her shoulders like a black velvet curtain.

When she looked in the mirror, she had second thoughts about the dress and was just wondering if there would be time to change, when the bell at the service door rang, announcing the arrival of the caterers. She would change after she had them settled, she promised herself.

Cle was not conceited, but she would have had to be blind not to have noticed the admiring glances coming her way from the two men who were setting out the food. Rather than feeling flattered, she was more determined than ever to change.

When she saw that things were in good shape she left the two men and hot footed it toward the bedroom. Before she had even crossed the hall, though, the front door bell was ringing. Cle sighed and answered the door.

"Darling, you look sensational," Jaime declared, taking hold of her arm and turning her in front of him. He looked at Max Brainerd, satisfaction on his face. "This is called 'Venus.' Lovely, isn't it?"

"Lovely, but the model is even lovelier," Max said, not bothering to hide his admiration as he looked her over from head to toe.

"I was just going to change . . ." Cle began.

"Ridiculous!" Jaime roared. "You look beautiful. My dress has made you so. You must wear it. I insist." Jaime quick-marched her into the lounge, where one of the white-coated young men was setting up a portable bar.

Still with his hand clutching Cle's upper arm, Jaime stalked to the bar and ordered a vermouth on the rocks, glaring at the hapless young man when he fumbled and put dry vermouth into the glass. Jaime liked sweet vermouth and assumed that everyone knew that.

"Jaime, will you be patient and let him get set up first?" Cle hissed, trying to pry his fingers from her arm. "And will you let go of me? My arm is going numb."

"First you will promise me that you won't change your gown! Oh, Max, answer the door, will you?" He turned back to Cle, his voice squeaking more than usual. "Promise you won't change."

"I promise, you tyrant." Cle watched him go back to the bar and begin badgering the bartender. "Jaime, there's something I have to tell you. Oh, yes, thanks for the Perrier." Irritated Cle put one hand on his arm and shook it. "Will you listen to me for a moment? I must tell you something."

Jaime looked past her, putting his professional smile in place. "No time now, for a tête-à-tête, Cleora, your guests are here," Jaime whispered from the side of his mouth.

Cle turned to greet the Nivenses and the Murrays and

the Bells. Cle had asked Diana Nivens if it was all right to invite the two couples she had met at their beach party and Diana had consented with enthusiasm, delighted that Cle had taken to Pam and George Murray and Ginna Bell. In the flurry of introductions of Jaime to the new arrivals, Cle had no time to pull him aside to tell him that Dev was in Sydney—more, that he would be here tonight.

Max had brought two of his models with him and Alistair's assistant, Clive Beavens and his wife. As more people kept arriving, Max confessed he'd overextended the invitations.

"I felt that you wouldn't mind, Cle dear," Max announced, smiling at her gasp of dismay.

"How many are coming??" she asked in a small voice.

"Not to worry. There won't be more than thirty. Forty would be the outside number." He smiled and patted her cheek. "You'll like them, dear. All walks of life, don't you know."

"Max," Cle wailed. "I'm not sure I have enough food or even enough to drink..."

"Something wrong, darling?" Dev's hand was warm at her waist as he leaned down and kissed her shoulder. "You look devastating." The palm of his left hand lay flat against her stomach as he pulled her back closer to him.

Cle stood there, not even turning to look at him, her body feeling as though it was going through a mini electrocution. "I...I might not have enough food or drink." Her voice was wooden. "When did you get here? I didn't hear the bell ring."

"Didn't you?" Dev's breath feathered her cheek as he lowered his head to kiss her ear. Then he straightened and without releasing her, snaked his right hand round her body and extended it to the puzzled-looking Max. "Hello. I'm Dev Carstairs."

"Max Brainerd." Max took Dev's hand without enthusiasm, his face growing more suspicious.

"I'll talk to the catering people for you, darling," Dev announced and with a nod to Max and a light kiss on Cle's hair, he moved toward the kitchen.

"Who is that? Or would you rather I didn't ask?" Max had a crease between his brows.

Before Cle could answer Max, she spied Jaime marching across the room. She closed her eyes for a moment wishing for a rocket that would send her right out of the room. "I think your question will be answered in a moment." Cle tried to smile at Max as Jaime thundered to stop at her side.

"What in hell is he doing here? I thought you came to Sydney to get away from him? You might have told me that you had changed your mind, Cle. "Jaime machine-gunned the words at her.

"Cool down, old boy," Max said quickly. "Your face is turning purple and people are looking at us."

"Max is right, Jaime. Cool down or you'll spoil the party." Cle sighed. "I don't know how he found me. He showed up this afternoon. I tried to tell you when you arrived this evening, but I didn't have time."

"Hello, Toner. Happy New Year." Dev lifted his glass in mocking salute. Then he turned to look at Cle. "All taken care of, darling. More food and drinks will be coming." He looked back at Jaime. "I heard you ask Cle how I got here." He took another swallow of what Cle knew would be Irish whiskey, a little water, and no ice. "I put detectives on you Toner. They informed me that you had booked a flight to Australia. Nice touch flying from Toronto International." Dev's smile had ice in it.

Jaime's face turned a rich magenta, his mouth opening and closing. Before he could say anything, Cle clutched his hand.

"Jaime, it's time for dinner. Please." Cle let her nails dig into his wrist, finally making him look down at her, his face an angry mask.

Cle had planned on a sit-down dinner but when she went to the caterer's with her excuses, she found them all smiles and more than willing to set out a buffet. Cle wondered just how much Dev had paid them to make them smile like that at all the inconvenience. It stunned Cle when she saw the array of food that was set out in the dining room. Small trays were being placed here and there so that people could put their plates and silverware on them. To her surprise dinner was only a half an hour later than she originally planned.

She looked once at Dev and was infuriated when he raised his glass to salute her. Damn the man! He did everything well, even to saving her dinner party. Instead of feeling grateful Cle had the strongest desire to up end the ice bucket over his head!

Everyone seemed to think the picnic atmosphere of the dinner a nice touch and people were laughing and talking to one another in a warm way.

Cle took her tray of food and sat on a stool near Max and Jaime but her ear seemed to be tuned to every word that Dev said. It irritated her that Pam Murray and Ginna Bell seemed to gush over his every syllable.

"And you practice in America as well as Britain, Mr. Carstairs . . . I mean Dev?" Ginna simpered.

"No, my law practice is in Great Britain, but I do consulting for firms throughout the world. I find business consulting the greater challenge."

"It's practical to have houses in both London and New York. We are thinking of opening one up in the Far East soon, and, of course, Sydney would be a perfect spot for a base."

"Wonderful," Pam cooed, her voice an irritant to Cle. "Then we could see you all the time."

"True," Dev answered, making the ladies laugh.

Cle could hear a roaring in her ears and wondered if she were coming down with the flu.

"And did you have to take special studies to become

a consultant in the States, Dev?" Pam asked.

"I attended Harvard Law School and Wharton School of Business in order to further my understanding." Dev's quiet voice rang false to Cle's ear. "Further his understanding indeed!" she harrumphed to herself. The man had passed the New York State Bar Exam and had a slew of degrees, both British and American.

"Ohhh," the two women chorused. "How bright you must be."

At that Cle rose to her feet, almost tilting the plate from the tray table.

Jaime looked up at her, dabbing at his mouth with a napkin. "Going back for seconds, Cle?"

"Going to be sick, I think." Cle gritted her teeth.

"What, Cle?" Jaime raised his voice, making Dev turn toward him.

Cle swung back, feeling that she was in some kind of awful silent movie. "I just want to check the time and the preparations. We wouldn't want midnight to creep up on us and not have the champagne ready." Cle quickly turned her back, not wanting Jaime to see the sour look she was sure was twisting her face at that moment.

"I'll help you," Dev stated, rising to his feet and placing his napkin and plate on his tray.

Cle opened her mouth to tell him that she didn't need his help but the flicker deep in those green eyes was menacing. Cle looked at both Max and Jaime, who were in turn looking at Dev. She thought for a moment that Jaime was going to rise.

Dev put his hand on the other man's shoulder. "Stay where you are. No sense all of us running." His voice was bland, his eyes acid green. Jaime stayed where he was.

Cle whirled away, mumbling to herself as she headed for the kitchen. The caterers were arranging the dessert trays with an inviting array of French pastries. They informed her they would clear the main course soon and asked if they could leave then since they were expected elsewhere shortly after midnight. They told Cle they would pick up the rest of their things the next day if she would leave them in the service hall.

"Yes, of course I will. Can you tell me the amount of the bill for the extra food and drink so I can have a check ready for you tomorrow as well."

"Oh, that was taken care of by your husband, ma'am," the older man said. The caterers took the trays to the other room.

Cle rounded on Dev, lounging against the wall. "How did that man get the idea you were my husband?" she spat at him. As he opened his mouth to answer her, she forestalled him. "And don't think I'm going to let you pay for the extras, because I'm not." She held out her hand, palm upward." Give me the bill this instant."

"I'll give it to you at the end of the evening," Dev drawled walking to the counter area where trays filled with tulip-shaped crystal glasses stood ready to be filled with bubbly. He glanced at his watch. "It's eleven-fifteen, Cle. By the time every one has dessert it will be getting close to twelve." He grimaced. "Not that anyone will feel like anything after that meal. It was very good, darling."

Stung, Cle glared at him. "And I suppose that the Carstairs would never serve champagne to anyone on a full stomach."

Dev straightened, a sculpted look to his features. "I wasn't being snide, Cle. And for your information, champagne is served anytime . . ."

"I know that." She wanted to shriek at him, but it came out a low snarl. She was too afraid of the others hearing them.

"Then why the hell did you make a remark like that?"

"Why the hell did you make the remark you did?"

His body thrust forward. "For a haepenny I'd . . . I'd—"

"You touch me, Your Lordship," Cle ground out, temper flaming through her body.

Dev's hand shot out like a missile, pulling her hard against him.

The door leading to the service hall opened and one of the caterers came through. He paused there, a curious look on his face.

"Don't think this is the end of it," Dev hissed into her hair, then he released her. Walking toward the man, he made complimentary remarks on the food and service, ending "and of course we'll recommend you to our friends."

"You don't have any," Cle muttered childishly.

The man was busy with his pots and pans so he didn't hear her, but Dev turned to glare.

Before he could say anything to her, Cle went to the counter and lifted one of the glass-laden trays. She knew she would have to return to the kitchen for the champagne but fear and a desire to make a flashy exit drove her to the lounge area.

Most of the people there were watching the television. A man was promising a minute-by-minute countdown to the new year as Cle placed the glasses on a table. She was about to ask Max if he would mind getting the champagne when Dev stepped close to her back. He was carrying several bottles and a linen towel. He put everything down on the table and with a minimum of effort he uncorked the first bottle and began filling the glasses. "This isn't New York State Champagne, Cle." One black brow arched.

"I'm settling for French," she snapped, lifting two of the glasses and handing them to the two models named Sandy and Lee.

Before she could take more from the tray, Ginna was there.

"Oh, Cle dear, let me help. You see to your guests. I'll be Dev's wine waiter." Ginna beamed up at him.

"Why thank you, Ginna." Dev's smile had a sensuous curve.

Cle turned away almost bumping into Diana Nivens. "Oh, sorry. The closer it gets to midnight, the clumsier I get." She forced a smile.

"You mustn't mind Ginna and Pam. They love to flirt and let's face it, Dev Carstairs is the best looking thing to hit Sydney in two decades."

Cle could feel heat in her face. "It has nothing to do with me how many women Dev has. He and I are just . . . acquaintances." The lie was like a wad of gum in her mouth.

When a glass of champagne was pushed into her hand, she took a sip at once.

"Don't gulp that stuff, darling. I'd rather not have to pick you up off the floor at your own party," Dev crooned into her ear.

Cle rounded on him, sputtering. "How like you to remind me of a very embarrassing incident . . ."

"Sickening, too, as I recall." He smiled down at her.

Cle gasped. "You're a rat, Devon Carstairs." She muttered an oath and took another gulp of champagne, then seeing Diana's curious glance, she almost choked. She debated with herself if she would go over and explain to Diana that the antipathy between Dev and herself was a long-standing family feud, when he took her arm and turned her closer to him. She looked up at him, still angry.

"The announcer says we only have two minutes." Dev's smile had a hard twist to it. "And you are staying with me."

Cle was trying to think of an argument, trying to steel herself against the pleasure that was mounting in her because Dev had his arm about her, when someone yelled "Happy New Year."

Dev took the glass from her hand and set it with his on a table. Then as though he had all the time in the world he enfolded her against him, tightened his hold at her token struggle, then let his mouth drop to hers like a brand.

At the first touch, Cle was lost, so much so, that she wrapped her arms around his neck. Dev's hold lifted her to her toes, then off the floor.

Cle could hear the other voices, could sense their movements but nothing intruded. She was on another planet with Dev. Their mouths were hungry for each other, their hands and bodies clutching and straining to be together.

When Dev released her and lowered her back to the floor, Cle was dazed. She tried to focus on Dev, when she was yanked away from him by Max who embraced her and swung her away. Next Jaime took hold of her. Cle sensed an urgency in his kiss but she was still too bemused by Dev's touch to analyze it.

She felt she was being passed around like a package but was glad of the excitement, hoping it had diverted attention from her and Dev.

Everyone came together in a large, loosely formed circle and held hands to sing "Auld Land Syne." Dev was standing between Pam and Ginna, and the sight brought a taste as bitter as alum to Cle's mouth as she thought of him kissing those women. She resolutely turned away. Soon though, the strain of keeping her eyes away from Dev began to tell. Her head started to ache and she was glad when the first couples decided to leave.

Diana and Alistair insisted on helping to clean up and so did Max. All Cle's arguing that there wasn't much to do was to no avail. Jaime even helped by finishing a few of the cheese puffs left on a tray. He did accompany Max to the kitchen, carrying one champagne glass, and chattering all the while about a new process he was working on to develop a dye for polyesters.

There was no way Cle could politely ask Dev to leave while the others were there. She seethed when he gave her a big smile and began collecting empty champagne bottles.

"He probably hasn't done this much manual labor in years," she muttered under her breath. "No doubt he'll have a stroke when he realizes how he's demeaned himself." She gave a cruel swipe at a food tray with the cloth in her hand.

"For someone who is just an acquaintance, he sure acts like a buddy, doesn't he?" Diana purred next to her, wiping out an ashtray with a napkin.

Cle frowned at her new friend. "He's an insensitive ass, that's all." Cle smiled her brightest smile as Diana's mouth went wide with astonishment.

Her headache got worse and worse as she vowed frantically, *I will get over him! I will get over him!* All the while a second little voice pounded an incessant chant of "ha-ha-ha."

To her surprise, Dev made no fuss when it was time to go. He did not leave any earlier than any of the others, but he did go with the last of them. Cle wasn't even irritated when he announced at the last moment that he was going to visit her bathroom. It only took minutes.

By the time the apartment was empty, Cle's head was throbbing so badly that all she could think of was the routine she had to force herself to follow. First a soak in a hot tub to relax, then the two specially prescribed tablets to take, then a hot drink.

She staggered into the bathroom and ran the water, promising to sleep until noon tomorrow . . . today, rather, she reminded herself.

She took her time in the bath, breathing deeply in the steamy atmosphere. Even though the temperature was in the high seventies out of doors, and she was dreadfully uncomfortable, she had to go through with it. Then, with the towel wrapped around her, her wet toes curling on the tile floor, she reached for the tablets that she kept in the lacquered Chinese cupboard that was the same color as the tiles. She swallowed them and gulped the water, sighing. Now one more step. She would have to make herself a hot drink, then sleep, and her headache would diminish if not go away entirely. She only had one or two of these a year but if she didn't treat them at once, they would get progressively worse, finally making her nauseated and very ill.

When she came out of the bathroom, she fumbled in her dresser drawer for a cool nightie. She donned a sheer cotton that had the texture of silk and was just as transparent.

Doddering to the kitchen like a woman old before her time, she kept one hand clutched to her head. She had to hope it wouldn't explode before the capsules and hot drink did their work.

Groggy, she stared at the apparition in front of her.

"What are you doing here?" she asked Dev through lips as stiff as pasteboard.

He turned from the stove, a steaming cup in his hand. "Here you are, love, your hot drink. It's lemon, honey, and hot water. Just what you need." Dev inclined his head at her, his eyes widening as they roved her from head to foot.

"Get out of here," she rasped at him, nausea making her sway.

Dev was across the room in two strides. He put the cup down on the counter, then swept her up into his arms.

Cle was too weak to argue with him and her head lolled on his shoulder. "I'm never sick. Put me down at once."

"Don't lie. You get violently ill when you have one of your headaches. You haven't had one in ages. I hope you see the folly of leaving me. It's made you sick."

"Has not." Cle moaned as he put her down on the bed and went back for the hot drink.

Dev returned, lifted her, holding her about the shoulders while she drank. "There. Now you'll sleep. Don't worry. I'll take care of everything."

"Just go away. Please," she begged, then groaned and turned on her side.

Dev laughed. "Go to sleep, you ungrateful brat."

Dev's laugh had never had that shaved-rock sound before she thought. And then sleep took her.

CHAPTER *Five*

CLE DIDN'T WAKE refreshed but she did wake free of the headache. The noises that wakened her weren't the familiar ones that she had begun to associate with a Sydney commercial area. As she looked foggily at the clock and saw that it was past noon, she assumed the caterers were collecting the last of their things. God! She jerked to a sitting position, yawning. Was everything where they could find it?

She crawled out of bed, rushing to the bathroom to splash cold water on her face and rinse out her dry as dust mouth.

Still bleary eyed and fumbling with the tie on the cotton wrapper she'd slipped on, she started down the hall leading to the kitchen area. A thump from the second bedroom made her pause, frowning. What would the caterers have left in the bedroom?

Smothering another yawn, she pushed open the door and stopped. She gasped as she watched Dev carry an armful of suits toward the closet and hang them there. She must have made some sound because he turned to look her way as he hung the last suit.

"What... what are you doing?" Cle licked her dry lips, a horrid thought taking shape in her mind.

"These are my clothes." Dev's smile had all the charm of a placid demon. "I'm hanging up my clothes," he said in a measured tone as though he were talking to a mental incompetent.

"Then you can just damn well unhang them and get them the hell out of my apartment." Cle's voice was a high-pitched roar as she catapulted herself toward the offending jackets hanging in the closet.

Dev caught her around the waist before she could reach her target. "Can I assume that your headache is better this morning?" That hard smile was on his face again and making Cle feel as though she were doing a balancing act on a sword.

Of its own accord her body began melting toward Dev. Gritting her teeth, she looked up at him from the prison of his arms. "Get your hands off me and leave my apartment."

"No." Dev set her away from him, but banded her arms between his strong hands. "I'm staying, my love. I'm staying with you. And you can bloody well swear, rant, scream, rage, throw things. It won't matter. I'm not leaving."

"I'll call Jaime... and Max... and Alistair!" Cle gasped, her hands shaking, not with anger, but with a need to touch Dev. This weakness of hers inflamed her more.

"Call them, please." Dev's teeth bared in a smile that had all the winsomeness of a piranha. "It would give me great pleasure to change the color of the great Toner's eyes or to loosen your Max Brainerd's teeth. I would really like that type of exertion, dear Cle." He let go of her and moved toward his cases.

"You can't fight! Besides, it would be three against one. They would throw you out." Cle silently cursed the tremor in her voice.

He swung around. "Call them. Let's put it to the test, shall we?" The green ice of his eyes made the upward curve of his mouth look like Satan's grin.

"You can't stay here," Cle blustered. "Go back to England and Larren."

"So you remember me speaking of Larren? Of wanting to show it to you?" He spat the words at her over his shoulder.

"I don't want to talk about that." Her hands balled into fists as she watched him put shoe cases into the closet. "I want you out of here."

"No." All at once Dev was back across the room before she even guessed his intention to move. "Come along to the kitchen. I've fixed you a light breakfast. When you're through, I've arranged for us to have a picnic lunch delivered to us by the caterers. Then we're going to the beach. We'll do some surfing."

"You don't surf." Cle glared up at him as he marched her to the kitchen, her fingers trying to pry his from her arm.

"Of course I surf," Dev said, pushing her into a kitchen chair and getting a plate of toast from the stove.

"Oh, God!" Cle groaned, munching and glaring, munching and glaring. "I hope a shark gets you, but he'd probably spit you right up again and gag for an hour."

"My, my, aren't you complimentary this morning?" Dev observed, his face bland. "Tummy upset?" He looked interested.

"Yes . . . no . . . It's none of your business what my stomach is doing." She wanted to pierce him through with her fork. Instead she stabbed the helpless egg on her plate. "Where did you learn how to surf?" she mumbled still looking at her lacerated egg.

"When I attended Harvard some classmates and I took a long break in California. Then, when I was based in the States, I used to take vacations in Hawaii. The surf at Waimea is outstanding." Dev answered, his tones mild.

"Peachy for you."

"Yes, it was."

"Don't you be so damned friendly." Cle choked on a bit of egg then swallowed the hot coffee too fast, making her cough increase. "And don't you... dare...pat...me on the back." She glared at him through watering eyes. "You are to get out of this apartment."

"Don't be boringly repetitive, darling." Dev rose, clearing both his things and hers from the table, flabbergasting Cle who had never known him to pick up anything.

"And don't think you're fooling me with this helpful boy routine," she said darkly, following him down the hall to the bedroom area. "I haven't said I'll go, you know."

"You have a choice, love." Dev's tones were silky. "You can either walk by my side or I'll wrap you in towels and carry you over my shoulder like a laundry bag."

Cle drew herself up to her full height, wishing for once that Dev were five-foot-three instead of well over six feet tall. "You can't threaten me, buster. You had better remember your law about coercing people."

"So sue me, but if you aren't ready in ten minutes I *will* bundle you like a parcel." He turned to walk into the room that he had the nerve to call his, when he paused. "And don't bother trying any cutesy, Yankee tricks, because I'm through fooling with you."

"Don't you dare insult my New York Yankee heritage...you you...Limey you..." She finished by shouting because Dev shut the door in her face.

Cle went through several battle plans while she was getting into the jeans and halter top that would be suitable to wear to the beach. She decided that she would drown him. No jury would convict her! She'd probably receive a medal for getting rid of a public nuisance. She rolled her bikini into a towel and went to the door.

Dev was waiting for her. She steamed by him, chin in the air, not even speaking to him as they descended in the elevator.

She glared from him to the silvery black Porsche, wondering how the devil he had gotten the car in such a short time. She locked her teeth together to prevent herself asking him.

They rode in silence. The sun was so dazzling it hurt the eyes. The ocean and sky were a hot blue that both warmed and cooled the spirit.

To Cle's surprise there were few people at the beach Dev chose. "Are you sure it's all right to swim here? There are places along here where the currents are tricky. Alistair Nivens told me—"

He interrupted. "I've checked with several persons including your friend Nivens about this beach. It's considered safe, but it is also private. Come along. Let me take your hand. These rocks could be treacherous."

"I'll be fine on my own, thank you."

"Cle." His voice sounded like iron filings.

"Oh, all right."

When they reached the flat area of the beach and Cle would have jumped the last few feet from the rocks, Dev stopped her with a hand on her arm. He jumped first, put down the bag he carried and turned to her with his arms held out.

"Jump."

"I can get down myself." She felt suddenly breathless.

"Jump, Cle."

She did. His arms closed around her at once, her body was swung free of the rocks and was allowed to slide a short way down Dev's body. When they were face to face, nose to nose, and eye level, Dev stopped the downward movement of her body.

"I want a truce today," he growled softly, his breath touching her lips.

"Too bad about what you want," Cle squeaked, pressing her hands against his rock-like shoulders but having no luck in pushing him away.

"Do we stay like this? Or do you tell me that you're going to pull in your horns and mind your waspish temper?"

"Me, waspish?" Cle struggled harder. "What about your acid tongue, Mr. Attorney, sir?"

"We both try. Agreed?"

Cle let out a shuddering sigh and nodded, not looking him in the eye. "All right. It *is* a beautiful day."

"Good girl." Dev laughed. Before she could guess his intention, his mouth was clamped to hers. The kiss was short and hard. When he released her she would have staggered but Dev's arm was there. To Cle's eye he seemed totally unaffected by the kiss.

She wanted to punch him for kissing her—and ask him to do it again! God! The thought made her take off at a run toward the water, leaving Dev to gather up the things she had dropped.

Over her shoulder she saw him coming at a slower pace. She stopped, taking the beach bag from her shoulder. She looked around frowning, searching for a place to slip on her suit. There were no other people in sight. Still, there *was* Dev.

A cluster of rocks off to one side offered the most privacy. She walked toward them, swinging her beach bag in her hand.

"Don't bother changing there for my sake, darling,"

Dev drawled behind her. "I've seen your lovely form so many times. Remember?"

"I thought you wanted a truce today." Cle didn't look back, feeling the heat rise in her face at the thought of just how many times Dev had seen her nude.

"Get changed, Cle."

Rebelliously she stepped behind the rocks. "There's no way we can have a truce," she said to herself. "A double murder maybe, but not a truce."

Dev wasn't on the beach nor in the water. Cle guessed he'd gone back to the car to get the surfboards. She ran into the water, gasping at the first shock of cold then reveling in it. When Dev appeared with the boards, she quickly went back to shore. Some of the eagerness she had felt the first time she surfed infected her now. Together she and Dev paddled out.

He came close to her and signaled for her to turn and paddle gently. She nodded as he indicated the waves coming up behind them.

When she looked over her shoulder and saw the rollers coming at her, she knew that these were much bigger waves than the ones she had dealt with at the Nivens's beach.

Heart in her mouth, she realized all at once that Dev assumed her experience to be greater than it really was. How he would laugh if he knew that during her one day of surfing she had managed to stand fully upright only once.

Dev signaled her that the next wave would be the one they could take together. It looked like a watery building coming at her.

Cle wanted to shout "no," but instead she found herself nodding and beginning to paddle harder toward the beach that now seemed a hundred miles away. As she edged her knees up, her mouth went dry in the midst of all that roaring water. From her peripheral vision she could see Dev on his feet, bent and balancing, the board like a bronco beneath him. She could tell, though, that he was watching her.

The tunnel of water behind her sounded like a railroad train and made her knees weak. She gathered her courage and forced her body to straighten.

For unbelievable seconds she rode that water, her heart hammering in her throat, her hands flung out on either side of her, her knees bent. For milliseconds she thought she might be able to hold on, to ride it to the beach. Elated, she risked a glance at Dev, who was riding his board, body fully relaxed, but his face grim as he watched her. All at once her board flipped into a near vertical position as she lost the curl. She felt herself plowed down in the horrendous torrent. All her training in swimming didn't prepare her for this! Panic gripped her as she swirled in the foaming green depths. Yet the years of training did make her kick upward even as her body was trapped in the roiling vortex.

Something grabbed her and held on. Lungs bursting, white sparks exploding on black velvet behind her eyes, she was pulled upward and shoreward. Air! Blessed air. She didn't even fight it when the water rolled her over and over. She was able to lift her head up because Dev was holding her tight around the middle.

They were tossed onto the beach like so much flotsam, their boards riding shoreward just a few yards aways. When Dev swept her up into his arms and carried her to the blanket he had spread for them, his face looked carved from ivory, his tan gone sallow.

He came down with her to the blanket, not releasing her. "Are you all right?"

"Yes. Boy, those waves sure shave the rough edges, don't they?" She tried to smile but her lips were wobbly.

"Just how many times have you been surfing?" Dev's question sounded like his best courtroom approach.

Cle decided not to hedge after looking into those emerald eyes. "Once."

"And that was when you went with Brainerd to the Nivens's place? That was the time you talked about New Year's Eve?"

Cle felt she should have answered, "Yes, Your Honor," but she merely nodded.

Dev closed his eyes and sank back on his heels. When he opened them again, his eyes were an opaque green. "You could have died out there. Do you know that?" His throat moved as though it was trying to disgorge a stone.

Cle lifted her hand, touching his thigh. "But you saved me, Dev. I'm fine."

"You could have died out there," he repeated, his voice very hoarse and low.

Alarmed, Cle tried to sit up, but all at once Dev was on her, forcing her body down, his mouth pressed to her face his arms gripping her hard.

"Don't say anything," he rasped out. "Don't you say one damn thing."

When Dev finally released her, he flung himself backward on the sand, one arm over his face.

Feeling helpless, Cle lay there. His thigh was pressed to hers and she knew an urgent need for that warm body of his.

Dev sat up at last, his face still having a pewter cast under his tan. He looked out over the ocean for long moments.

Cle let her eyes touch his every pore, loving that firm-muscled body better than her own.

When he turned in a jerky motion to look down at her, she could feel the blood stealing up her neck and over her cheeks. He said nothing, just stared at her. He let out a long, whistled breath. "Are you sure you're all right?"

"Yes. I'm fine. Really I am." She wanted to wipe that bleak look from his face, thaw the green ice in his eyes.

He nodded once. "We'll have some fruit. I told the caterer to include those pink melons he brought to the party." Dev's smile looked static. It seemed to take him a long time to slice the melon, but Cle was sure that she was mistaken when she saw a tremor in his hand.

Dev kept feeding her more and more slices of melon until between the two of them, they finished it. They rested a while. Dev abruptly rose to his feet, brushing some sand from his thigh. He didn't look at her when he spoke. "Come on, Cle, we're going in again. This time I'll take you on my board until you get the feel of it."

Cle stood, looking at him, wondering if he was angry with her. "Fine with me."

His head swiveled toward her. "You're not afraid then?"

"No." Cle knew it was true. She would never be afraid as long as Dev was with her. Even as the thought mushroomed in her mind, she groaned to herself.

Cle followed him out into the water and as he gestured to her, she bellied down on his board, feeling his body on her legs. She tried to paddle in concert with Dev's strokes and was amazed at how rapidly they glided into deep water.

Dev turned them, then they were both looking over their shoulders as the waves rushed toward them. The one that Dev chose seemed small compared to some others but it was still a mountain of water to Cle.

His hands were at her waist. She marveled at the strength of his legs balancing both of them on the board until he had her in the proper crouch. As they entered the curl, Cle could feel Dev's feather touch guiding her stance. Exhilaration filled her as the board lifted and swept shoreward at an impossible speed. She and Dev were the only persons on the planet! The sound of her laughter was a whisper in the roar but it seemed Dev heard it because she felt those long fingers squeeze her waist.

As the board sagged shoreward, she sank down, falling off the board with Dev almost on the beach. "That was wonderful, marvelous..." She gasped, laughter bubbling in her.

Dev's smile was slow in coming but as his strong arm lifted her up, the other balancing the board, Cle saw the twitch of his lips.

"Let's do it again. Please, Dev." Cle lifted her arm and placed it on his bare back, trying to still the shiver that went through her at the touch.

"Of course we'll do it again." Dev's smile was real this time and the satiric drawl was just as familiar and bracing.

Dev took her out three more times with him before he would let her take her own board. When they paddled out together, her ears were filled with his instructions. He was right at her side.

The waves had been getting progressively bigger and Cle could see the crease of worry between Dev's brows as he scanned the waves behind them. Cle wanted to reassure him but the thunder of the water prevented conversation. Finally Dev signaled a wave and she began paddling, watching as Dev had instructed her. She rose in slow motion to her feet as she entered the curl, the feeling of excitement almost choking her. She rocked several times but managed to keep to her feet...then she was flying as the board lifted like a live thing and she sped toward the beach. Was there ever such a feeling before? Cle's mind reacted to what Dev had taught her, the thrill only seeming to sharpen her reflexes. She was doing it. She was riding the surf.

When she sank into the water, Dev was there, his hand on her at once, making her realize that somehow he had managed to ride with her all the way.

Dev called a halt for lunch. It was a lovely meal of cold prawns with a hot sauce, slices of chicken breast, fruit salad, dark bread, and small pieces of cake that Dev told her was called fruitcake in Scotland. To Cle it looked like flaky squares of pie dough with apples, raisins, and currants spread thinly between the layers. There was lemonade to drink and Australian beer that Dev told her tasted like good English ale.

Cle looked at him. "And you say that I'm such a Yankee. You should listen to yourself talking about Scottish things and English things. You brag more than I do."

Dev looked up at her as he reclined on one elbow with the bottle of beer in his hand, studying her as she knelt on the blanket. "I will never tease you about being a Yankee again. Not after today when I've seen such a display of Yankee courage."

Cle felt weak at his words, boneless, embarrassed yet delighted. "I . . . I wasn't brave. I was really very frightened."

"Yes. You were frightened but when I asked you to go back into the water with me, you didn't hesitate." He rose to a sitting position, bringing himself closer to her. "You Yankee ladies are something special, ma'am," Dev mimicked a Southern drawl.

"I'm glad you realize that, suh." Cle tried to match his mood; his nearness was making her giddy.

Even though Cle begged him, Dev wouldn't let her take the board out again. He said she was more tired than she realized. She started to argue with him. When the Carstairs jaw jutted forth, she gave up. It was a waste of time . . . and breath. Dev was capable of throwing her over his shoulder and carting her to the car. Besides she did feel a strange lassitude.

"It's a delayed reaction." Dev said as he entered the car and sat sideways watching her, her head lolling against the back of the seat.

Cle turned her head slowly. "Don't be silly. I'm strong as an ox."

Dev leaned over, his lips feathering her cheek before they clamped with the gentlest pressure on her mouth. "You have the heart of a lion . . . true, but you still suffered a trauma. It will be warm milk, an omelet, a soothing bath, and bed for you as soon as we get home."

"English aristocrats sure are bossy." Cle's eyelids fluttered. "Especially *lords.*" She couldn't lift her lids.

"Right. And don't you forget it." His mouth pressed her lids tighter shut.

When Dev lifted her from the car, she mumbled that she was too heavy, that she had had enough sleep in the car and now she could walk. Still she was so glad when he muttered something about not being so stubborn and held her tight in his arms.

She could remember telling him that she was sorry she had slept all the way home from the beach as he removed her clothes, then lifted her into a tub of water that seemed to make her even sleepier. She yawned hugely in Dev's face as he used the loofah sponge on her stomach and breasts. "Ummm?" She muttered when she heard him curse about bruises. Cle wondered for a hazy moment where his bruises were.

He wrapped her in a fluffy bath sheet that covered her from neck to ankle. She smiled when she heard him chuckling about not being able to dry her when she kept sagging against him like that. She heard her own long, satisfied sigh when he placed her between the sheets. She tried to open her eyes when he said something about forgetting the omelet for the time being.

Cle had a hazy awareness of something warm embracing her body. She snuggled closer, contented. Sleep was falling down a black, quiet well.

She awoke once in the night, fuzzily aware of contentment and a feeling of security. There was something that wasn't quite right and she knew that if she concentrated it would come to her what it was, but that sense of contentment was too strong. She fell back into the cocoon of sleep.

Sunlight performed a macabre arabesque on the ceiling. Cle blinked at it for long moments letting the puzzle pieces of her mind take shape, then assemble.

She stiffened at the familiar warmth at her back. Her eyes blinked once, twice, three times. Yes, she was awake. She wasn't dreaming again about being with Dev back in the apartment in New York. No, it was real! She was awake! It was still a holiday because New Year's Day had been Saturday this year. Today was Sunday, she catalogued in perspiring dread, not wanting to turn around and see that face, not wanting to look down and see that arm around her waist, knowing if she did that arm would be coated by dark hairs, that the skin would be tanned. My God, she thought, if he wakes up right now, he'll make love to me and I'll not only let him, I'll beg him to. Cle groaned to herself, hating her weakness. Damn him to hell! She hoped when he did marry *the right woman,* she'd have a nose like the London Bridge, a face like the map of Scotland, legs like London lamposts, and hips like the gates to Buckingham Palace.

Gritting her teeth, Cle readied her body for flight, knowing that if Dev were awake his reflexes wouldn't give her a second chance to escape his hold. With a feather touch she lifted the sheet, then catapulted out of the bed. As her feet hit the floor she was running for the bathroom. She heard the rustle and thump behind her and knew that Dev had made a grab for her. She slammed the door, locked it, and took deep, long breaths as she leaned against it.

"Don't be too satisfied with yourself, darling," Dev crooned from the other side of the door, making her leap away from the wood as though it had just caught fire. "You have to come out of there sometime."

"Are you set on raping me?" Cle squeaked, reaching for a towel and cuddling it to her like a security blanket.

"You know damn well it wouldn't be rape between us, Cle." Dev's voice hadn't risen, but there was a thread of steel in it.

"I'm not staying in here like a prisoner. When I come out of here if you touch me, I'll call the police."

"Don't get hysterical, love. You know I'd never threaten you. Take your bath, then come out. I'll get breakfast ready."

"Dev, wait." Cle went closer to the door. "I'm supposed to go to Max Brainerd's today for cocktails and a buffet at four . . ."

"I know. I've already been invited. We'll go together."

"We can't," Cle wailed into the wood of the door.

"Do you still keep your phone numbers in a drawer in the kitchen?" Dev's peremptory tone threw her off.

"Yes," she answered without thinking. "Dev? Dev, are you there?" She listened at the door for a moment, then decided that he had left the bedroom. Shrugging, she turned to her bath, then looked at the shower and back to the bath. Shower! Yes! That's what she'd do then she could shampoo her hair at the same time.

She smiled at the thought that at that moment in New York people would be walking in snowstorms, slush, and sleet while here there was hot sunshine in January. She mumbled to herself as she stepped under the cool shower. And if she didn't stop talking to herself this way, she'd be wheeled into the white wagon and driven away.

Again Dev shocked her by preparing a perfect omelet for breakfast. The coffee was black and rich, the toast crisp and oozing with butter. She looked at him, suspicion uppermost in her mind. "Bucking for head chef at McDonald's?" she asked sweetly, taking a big sip of the hot coffee.

"I thought you'd be pleased that I was multi-talented."

"You know darned well that you never once cooked when we were in our . . . that is *your* apartment in New York."

"Mrs. Hubbard would have been hurt," he said as he scooped more of the omelet onto their plates, then served wedges of crisp broiled tomatoes.

Silence reigned while they ate. Cle couldn't help the "ummm" of pleasure that escaped as she forked the food into her mouth. She glared at Dev when he smiled in satisfaction.

"About tonight—" Cle dabbed at her mouth with a napkin then reached for her coffee cup as Dev gestured with the pot.

"Don't worry about this afternoon and tonight." Dev smiled, his teeth reminding her of a crocodile. "I called Brainerd's place and told him that I would be taking you." He poured coffee into her cup, careful not to spill it when the cup jerked in her hand.

"You have a nerve telling them that when I told them that. . . . Oh, God . . ." Cle blanched. "Did you tell them where you were calling from?"

Dev didn't answer her but his crocodile smile widened, making Cle want to pour her coffee down his shirt.

CHAPTER
Six

AS THE DAY wore on, Cle's anger increased. She went looking for Dev, bound and determined to have it out with him. She found him in the bathroom off his bedroom scrubbing the tiles. "Dev, this charade has gone far enough. Your blue-blooded family would turn purple with rage if they could see you now." She stood there arms akimbo, her anger out of all proportion. She wanted to tilt the scrub bucket over his head. She wanted to take the brush and ram it between those even rows of teeth now widened in a smile. "Now you get off that floor and get out of here."

"I thought you said that we couldn't—"

"I never said *we,* not once!" She inhaled an angry breath as he slowly uncoiled his length and stood, dwarfing her, dwarfing the bathroom. She lifted her chin, forcing herself to look into those green eyes. "I want to talk to you." She sniffed, turning her back on him and starting to move away. "Right now. In the lounge," she stated, still moving away.

Inhaling, she marched to the lounge area, turning to take a stance in front of the fireplace. Her resolve wobbled a bit when Dev was nowhere to be seen.

By the time he strolled into the front room, her rock-hard speech had a melting, jello-like consistency. "Where did you go?" she squealed at him.

The dark arch of eyebrows rose, the green eyes were emerald fire. "Why I washed up a bit, love. Did you miss me?"

"Yes . . . No, of course, I didn't. I want to talk to you."

Dev ambled to her side, took her arm and sat her down next to him, his thigh alongside hers, one of his arms stretched along the back of the couch. "So you said." He smiled down at her, then leaned toward her, a crease in his forehead as one finger came up to swipe at her cheek. "Smudge."

"Stop that." She tried to move away but Dev's arm came down to her shoulder, holding her. When she found that she couldn't budge him, she turned to face him, looking at his chin. "You can't stay here any more. I don't want a roommate and I don't want people talking about me."

"That didn't bother you in New York." Dev leaned toward her, his breath feathering her cheek.

"That's different. Nobody talks about anybody in New York," Cle argued lamely, trying not to think about that warm breath near her ear. "I don't know what people think here in Sydney and I have no intention of starting off on the wrong foot."

"To use your sweet Yankee phrase, 'Balderdash,'" Dev said, speaking absently.

"That's not Yankee. It's English." Cle almost whimpered.

"Is it? Whatever." Dev hitched his body closer, his fingers dancing on her shoulder. She felt a tingle—even through the cotton of her long-sleeved working shirt. "Your problem is that you fight the inevitable, Cle, darling."

"No such thing. I just don't want you here."

"Yes, you do. You want me here. I want to stay here. I'm going to stay here."

"What about your work? You were swamped with work when we were in New York. What about International Soft Ware? Triad Digitronics? You said that you had to handle them personally." Cle's voice wavered.

"So I did. The sooner we get back to New York, the sooner I'll be able to handle them personally again, too." Dev crooned the words into her ear.

"I'm not going back to New York." Cle gulped, trying to keep her body stiff.

"Then I'll handle it with a few phone conferences." Dev's index finger traced her cheek. "I've been talking to people we've worked with before out here and they seem eager to merge an office with ours. It would be good business on both sides."

"I won't be manipulated."

"No. You generally manipulate me," Dev observed.

"Me? You're insane. When have I ever tried to manipulate you? Not once. Admit it." Not giving Dev a chance to reply even as he opened his mouth to do so, she rushed on. "And even if I tried, what a joke that would be. Can you just see Lord Carstairs being pushed around by me?"

Dev's warm look hardened, but when Cle would have backed away, his arm tightened on her shoulder. "You seem to be a tiny bit obsessed with *Lord* Carstairs, my love. No matter how often I have told you to forget that part of me you continue to bring it up. Can it be that you have a fancy to be *Lady* Carstairs?"

Cle could feel her mouth opening and closing, like

a gaffed fish. "How dare you? What a fool you are to say such a thing. I am an American citizen and that's good enough for me. Now you let me go and don't you ever say such a thing to me again." Cle shoved at him with a determined effort, rocking him back enough to free herself. She jumped to her feet and turned to face him. "You're a conceited ass. You belong with Lady Clare and Clive and all those other phonies and even though I was your damned *mistress* for want of a more modern word, I'd never be your damned wife. Do you think I'd sit still for you getting tired of me, listening to your friends laugh about your 'Yankee' and laughing with them. . . . Well, you can think again, Dev Carstairs. I wouldn't have you if you were gold plated." A shuddering sob shook her. She swung away at a run. When she reached her room, she slammed the door behind her.

Standing in the middle of the room, both fists pressed to her mouth, she cursed Dev, she cursed herself for loving him. "He's a sadist, a sadist. How dare he mention marriage to me knowing that he didn't mean it? How could I ever think that I could love such a man? God, I hate him." She threw herself face down on the bed. She wouldn't cry. She would never cry about Dev Carstairs. She would root him out of her life. She would stomp his memory to death.

She had no idea how long she slept, but when she woke she had the feeling that she was on a sinking boat. She felt smothered in water. The motion of the boat rocked her body back and forth. She lifted her head from its place deep in the pillow and the smothering feeling went away. Hands at her waist turned her onto her back and the rocking sensation stopped. It had been Dev shaking her awake. She looked up at him through the wool of sleep.

"Time to get dressed, Cle." His voice was soft but there was a reserve to it that Cle recognized. Dev was behind his British barrier where none could penetrate.

"You look like a little girl with the sleep still in your eyes. I don't think you'll ever be old." The smile changed and he leaned back. After a few moments he rose and crossed to the door, closing it softly behind him.

She decided to wear a strapless blue cotton street-length dress. She peeled off her clothes and put on the cotton wrap she wore to apply makeup. She was finishing her face, adding a touch of pink gloss to her lips, when Dev walked into the room without knocking. "Leave," she said hoarsely.

He ignored the command. "Toner called again. I told him to get back to the States fast. If he persists in coming around you, I'll break his damned neck for him." He pivoted and left the room.

Cle looked at her openmouthed image, the streak of lipstick running upward from the corner of her mouth where her startled hand had smeared it. Wiping viciously at the mark, she wondered how she ever had imagined that she could love a despot? How could she have ever thought that that dry land piranha who stood six feet plus was charming? Witty? More sexy than any other man in the world? She was going to see a good psychiatrist as soon as possible!

She slipped into the pale blue strapless dress. It was cotton but had the feel of silk. The wrap around style with a Spanish ruffle hem that just touched the knee was more attractive on than it looked on the hanger. She wore slings in pale blue hopsacking with high wooden heels. She stared at her twin in the mirror. Who would have thought such a simple looking cotton could have such a daring effect? She complimented Jaime for the clever mind's eye that allowed him to see a creation totally before he put it to paper, much less to needle and thread.

She put tiny dot pearls into her ears. She was ready. Now if she could only find a matching baby blue .357 magnum pistol, she'd be perfectly outfitted! For a moment her wry humor failed her and she wallowed in self-pity as she pictured her struggle to keep Dev from knowing of the emotional stranglehold he had on her.

When she strolled into the lounge, she wasn't conscious that she had taken the model's stance as a type of inner self-defense. Jaime had taught her to use that pose if a customer made her very nervous.

Dev was standing at the bar in the corner, a short glass of deep amber liquid swirling from the absorbed motion of his hand.

Probably plotting my murder, Cle thought, taking a breath and stepping down to the lounge.

Her sound or movement must have penetrated Dev's deep thoughts, because he turned, his head lifting to look at her in the same motion. Those green eyes lasered her from toe to eyebrow.

Cle saw the tightening of his lips, the white bracketing of his mouth but he only inclined his head.

"Ready?"

"Yes."

He gestured for her to precede him out of the apartment, then he followed her into the lift, punching the button with a force that could have broken the circuit.

The car ride was punctuated only by the traffic noises around them. Cle had the feeling that Dev could hear every painful swallow she made.

Max's place was a very modern high-rise apartment that had a view of the ocean and was reached by an outside elevator. She longed to make some remark on the beauty of the Sydney waterfront but Dev's closed look forestalled any small talk.

She breathed a sigh of relief when the door to the apartment was flung open and Max's smiling face was there. He took one quick look at them, then pulled Cle into a loose embrace, ignoring Dev's hostile glance.

"Why don't you tell 'Sir Dark Looks' to get lost," Max whispered before he released her.

Cle smiled, saying nothing, but catching sight of

Jaime standing in the center of the room. Two women were hanging on his every word. She homed in on him, not looking left or right as she crossed to his side.

Jaime's professional look of boredom was in place. When he saw it was Cle, he started for a moment, the mask of ennui slipping. "What in hell? Oh!" Jaime bowed at the two women. "If you'll excuse me, ladies."

The women looked at Cle with active dislike for plucking their prize from them.

Jaime gripped Cle's arm above the elbow and steered her toward the bar. "You look lovely in my dress, my gorgeous deceiver. You have *some* explaining to do."

Cle accepted the drink Jaime handed to her, hoping he had remembered to make it non-alcoholic. She sipped the seltzer laced with lime and sighed with pleasure. She felt like lifting out one of the ice cubes and rubbing it on her forehead. Apparently Max's air conditioning wasn't working.

"You looked flushed, Cle." Jaime looked at her with disfavor. "You should think cool as I do. I told Max to turn off the air conditioning. It's poisonous for the lungs, you know."

"Jaime, you're outrageous, telling Max what to do in his own home." Cle pushed a breath of air upward from her mouth trying to cool her face, succeeding in lifting a few tendrils of hair from her warm forehead. She blessed the thought that had made her change her mind and twist her hair into a knot in back. She was glad they had walked out onto the small semicircular balcony with a beautiful view of Sydney and the ocean. There was a blessed breeze.

"Cle, stop pussyfooting around!" Jaime exclaimed as she leaned over the railing and inhaled the cool breeze. "What the hell possessed you to let Carstairs move into the apartment? Are you out of your tiny mind? I thought you wanted to be rid of the man."

Cle turned her head away from the sights and looked

at Jaime's pinched face. "I didn't want him to move in. He just did it. I *do* want to be rid of him and I'm going to get rid of him." She took a long drink of the seltzer. "How to do it is what has me flummoxed," she mumbled.

"We'll call the police and have the bastard ejected." Jaime was incensed. "Do you know that he told me to stay out of your life, that he said he would punch me in the nose if I didn't stay away from you?"

Cle laughed. "Jaime, you're exaggerating. Dev would never threaten . . ." Her voice trailed off as she remembered Dev coming to her room. "I'll break his damned neck for him," he'd said. And that wasn't his first threat to Jaime and Max. Cle looked at Jaime blankly. "Maybe he's going through change of life." She immediately wondered what ever made her say such a stupid thing. Dev was having an awful effect on her. She was acting like a drunk or a druggee and she neither drank nor took drugs. He was a menace, a sharp-tongued enemy of her peace of mind.

"Cle? Cle, come out of your daydream." Jaime shook her arm until she looked at him. "Come with me, I have something to show you." He didn't wait for her response, but pulled her after him. They reentered the room, now overflowing with people, some of whom Cle recognized. With a hot stab she watched Dev incline his head, smiling, toward a beaming Ginna Bell. She turned away fast and followed Jaime blindly from the room and down a short hallway.

The noise was muted in the bedroom areas and without the press of people, it seemed several degrees cooler.

Jaime closed the door behind them and pulled a large portfolio from the closet. He opened it on the bed.

All Cle's firm intentions to stay near the open window disappeared when she saw the colorful sketches that spilled from the case. "Jaime! These are something!" She gasped as she sank down next to him on the bed and took a sketch from his hands. "Wait a minute." Cle rummaged through her purse until she found her granny glasses, settling them on her nose.

"Lord, Cle, you look like a librarian." Jaime sniffed. "Whatever made you adopt such an unattractive affectation?"

She made a face at him, then looked back at the sketch in her hand. "It's not an affectation. Max took me to his eye doctor. The doctor suggested this prescription to prevent further eyestrain. I like them."

"Fool."

Cle ignored him. "This line will be a hit, Jaime. I love your uses of satin . . . here . . . and here."

Jaime sounded smug as usual. "All my lines are good, of course, but I do think this one has excessive panache. Remember the day you wanted a dress for a dinner you were attending with Carstairs?" As Cle nodded, grimacing, he added, "Yes that was the time you got so roaring drunk, dear Cleora."

Cle pushed at him and Jaime out of balance fell back on the bed, just missing the sketches. Cle leaned over him, one fist shaking in his face, laughter bubbling in her. "I was not *roaring* drunk, you—"

The door crashed open behind her and Cle swiveled her head, a startled look on her face. Jaime raised his head from where he reclined so that now he and Cle were much closer.

Dev stood there, his face working as though every muscle had turned to grinding stone. The movement up and down his throat looked forced and painful, his eyes were a leaping green fire. "Get off that damned bed, Cle." The measured words were more menacing than if they had been shouted.

She looked at him, not moving, her hand still curled into a fist, scarcely recognizing the man who stood in the crouched fighter's stance in the doorway. Coming to life, she jumped to her feet, looking down at a goggle-eyed Jaime who was not trying to sit up, then back to

Dev whose hands opened and closed in spasmodic rhythm. "What do you think you're going to do?"

"I'm going to take him apart," Dev said.

Cle yelped and moved, until she was standing at the end of the bed, between a just-rising Jaime and a bullish Dev. "Don't you dare say such a thing, Dev Carstairs. What's the matter with you? Have you gone completely crazy?" She was torn between a desire to scream at him and a need not to let the other people in Max's apartment know what was going on. "Dev, do you have a few slices missing in your loaf? Just where do you get off following me into this room and—"

"Bedroom. Call it what it is, a *bed*room," Dev growled, his eyes shooting at her like green rockets, then fixing right back on Jaime. "Now get out of the way. I'm going to teach your little dressmaker a lesson. Then I'll take care of—"

"Dressmaker!" Jaime roared, leaping from the bed and pushing around Cle, who tried to hold him back. "Why you insufferable English snob, where do you get off calling anyone names? You and your pompous friends . . . We'll see who will pull who . . . whom . . . Oh damn. Just let me get my hands on Little Lord Fauntleroy . . ." Jaime's voice was loud enough to shatter glass and no amount of shushing on Cle's part was having an affect.

She turned to face Dev when she heard him snarl, knowing that neither man had any control at the moment. She had a vision of her body being sandwiched between the two angry men as she saw Dev thrust forward and felt Jaime jostling at her back. Dev put out his hands to lift her out of the way when all at once he was pulled backward. The surprise on his face would have been ludicrous if Cle had been able to feel anything but relief at the sight of Max and Alistair grimly clutching Dev's arms.

Dev struggled with them and for a moment it looked

like he would throw the two of them down when all at once he subsided, his eyes like a death ray on Cle. "Let me go. I'm not going to do anything. I've decided that it isn't worth spoiling a party." He kept his eyes on Cle.

For no reason that she could name, a blush stole up her neck and face. She had done nothing to earn that look in Dev's eyes. She could easily have strangled him at that moment, relishing the thought of his neck between her hands. How dare he sit in judgment of her!

Dev looked at Jaime. "Get back to New York where you belong. The next time we meet, I'll make sure we're alone."

"You don't dictate to me," Jaime said, outraged, his face contorted. "And I'll look forward to meeting you again."

"No more of this," Max insisted, his lips a straight line as he looked from the men to Cle who sagged against the bed post.

Dev shook off the restraining hands and looked at Max. "I'm sure you'll understand if I don't stay. Of course, I apologize for causing a disturbance at your party."

"Of course," Max said, his face as taut as Dev's. "I'll see to it that Cle gets home all right."

"She isn't going back to that apartment with him in it," Jaime squawked, not listening when Alistair told him to be quiet.

She wasn't sure if Dev heard Jaime, but at least he didn't return, so she assumed that he left. It took long moments for Max and Alistair to calm Jaime down, but finally he was induced to return to the party. She would have liked nothing more than to remain where she was . . . in the bedroom. She didn't want to go home where Dev might be and she didn't want to face Max's guests.

"It won't be bad, Cle," Alistair whispered. "I really don't think too many people realized what was happening. Max and I heard Jaime yelling when we went to the kitchen to get beer for some of the men." He patted her on the back. "It's nothing to worry about. Even the best of men get into an altercation now and then."

"Yes. I suppose so," she answered him, trying to smile. But not Dev Carstairs, cool business head, cold solicitor's logic filling his brain. What was happening to Dev?

The rest of the party was an ordeal for Cle but it seemed what Alistair said was true. The only ones who seemed affected by Dev's absence were Ginna and Pam.

"I thought you came with Dev, Cle," Ginna said, a sour look on her face.

"I did," Cle said, wondering if her makeup were cracking on her face, it felt so stiff.

"Was it business?" Pam's face quivered with curiosity.

"I suppose," she hedged.

"I find him fascinating." Pam sighed. "He said he would come to dinner one evening when he was free." Her smile when she looked at her friend Ginna had a triumphant lift.

"Nice for you," Cle observed, moving away.

She was grateful when the Nivenses suggested that they leave.

Once in the car, Diana turned to her. "Alistair told me what happened. Would you like to spend the night at our place, Cle? We have plenty of room."

Cle shrugged. "I'm not worried about going home. Dev does not hit women. Believe it or not, he is a very *un*violent man."

"Just a man who happens to be very possessive of a certain woman," Alistair observed drily.

"Yes," Cle said biting her lip.

The drive took mere minutes it seemed to Cle, for despite her assurances to the Nivenses, she was uneasy about going into the apartment. Not because she was afraid that Dev would hurt her, she was afraid that they would have another argument and she knew she wasn't up to that.

Alistair saw her to the elevator, checking to see that it was empty before he let her enter.

Cle commented that he seemed to have all the canniness of a New Yorker as she shook his hand goodnight.

"We have some criminals here, too." He smiled at her, then he looked serious. "Are you sure you're all right?"

She nodded and stepped into the empty elevator. The hum of the motor seemed loud as she climbed upward. She put her key into the door and it swung open before she could return it.

Dev stood there, a drink in his hand.

Cle could tell by the glitter in his eyes that it wasn't his first drink.

"Yes, I've been drinking, my lovely temptress, but I am by no means drunk." He took another swallow and watched her as she walked by him.

"Drink yourself into a stupor, if you wish." She turned to face him. "But make sure you're sober enough to pack your things tomorrow. I want you to leave."

"No, my pet, I'm not leaving. I'm not only not leaving your flat, I am not going to leave your side . . . ever again." His tones had a slight slur but Cle knew he had a hard head and that booze rarely bothered him.

"I'm not going to fight with you on this. I'm going to bed. Just make sure you're out of here tomorrow."

"I bloody well won't leave," Dev grated out, then swung away striding toward the lounge and not looking back.

Cle rushed to her bedroom. She threw off her strapless cotton and headed for a cold shower. Instead of singing in the shower, she shouted. "That man is impossible. What does he want from me? I don't have to put up with this. I'll tip him out a window!"

She slept fitfully, having dreams about facing Dev in the bullring. No matter what she did with her red cape, Dev always seemed to come crashing through the middle.

By the time she woke up the next morning she had a giant headache. "How ironic," she said aloud as she sat up in bed, holding her head. "You have a hangover and you didn't drink." She swung her legs to the floor. "If Dev doesn't have a hangover, I should hit him over the head just to get him started. That war-like Limey is the cause of my headache." She was still muttering as she put on a cool turquoise cotton scooped-necked dress that left her arms bare. She wore flat-heeled sandals of natural rope and a natural rope shoulder bag that was big enough to carry all she needed for a day at Max's salon.

To her surprise Dev was in the kitchen drinking orange juice. A Palm Beach suit in champagne silk set off his deep tan. His face had a pallor and there were lines under his eyes but he looked alert, cool, and successful.

"I thought you would be sound asleep after your cuddle with the bottle," she said as she poured herself some juice.

"Did you?" Dev walked toward the doorway leading to the hall. "I have a business dinner this evening so I won't be home until late."

"Fine." Cle ground her teeth when she heard the front door slam. "Why didn't I tell him to get lost? Why do I put up with him?" Because you love him, the gleeful inner voice answered her. "How can I continue to love a man who wants to take over all my life but not really want me in his?" He never said that, the voice insisted. She felt as though someone had held a lit cigarette to her skin.

She shut everything else from her mind and went to work. The salon was teeming with activity. Max had decided to whip his spring show—which would be like Jaime's fall show—into shape early enough in the season so that he could eclipse some of his rivals in design. Jaime had generously offered to help him.

When Cle was working in the big design studio, bent over her drawing board, Jaime came to talk to her.

"Are you angry with me, Cle?"

She looked up, smiling at his pixie face. "No, I'm not angry with you, Jaime. I'm not angry with anyone, but I feel drained and I've made up my mind that I'm not going to be pushed into another situation like that if I can help it."

Jaime leaned over and kissed her cheek. "I don't blame you." He squinted at her. "I think I remember telling you that Carstairs was not good for you?"

"Please, Jaime, let's not rehash. I'm not in the mood."

"Well, are you in the mood for hearing that I'll be heading back to New York in three days?"

She put down her sketching pen. "Not because of what happened?"

"No, because I have a great deal of work to do."

She smiled at him.

"Cle, come home if it gets too rough here. I'll take care of you. I want to do that. I've wanted to do that for a long time. We work well together. We get along. You don't have to stay here the full two years. Come home and I'll take care of you."

She felt the sting of tears as Jaime put his arm around her.

CHAPTER Seven

CLE COULD NEVER remember a time when she and Dev remained more silent with each other. There had always seemed so much to say to one another that they would have burst if they hadn't told one another. Now it was different. Neither would speak unless it was absolutely necessary. Dev seemed to be gone more in the evenings. Cle was both glad and furious when this happened. She tried to work late as many nights as she could. Mornings she timed her breakfast so that there would be the least chance of seeing him.

On the day that Jaime returned to the United States, Cle went to the airport with him, borrowing Max's gleaming Mercedes sedan to freight Jaime's luggage.

"Come home with me, Cle," Jaime urged, as he felt in his pockets for his passport, finally hauling it out to show Cle. "See, I told you I hadn't forgotten it." He put it away then looked at her frowning. "Will you come home now?"

"No." Cle smiled, feeling strained. "That would be leaving Max in the lurch."

"Promise me you'll come if Carstairs becomes more bothersome." He looked like a petulant elf as Cle, listening to the announcement of the boarding for his flight, pushed him toward the security area.

It was no surprise to Cle that the alarm went off when Jaime tried to pass through. What stiffened her spine and made her surge forward was when she saw Jaime glare at the offending alarm, then swell with indignation when the girl monitoring the equipment asked him to step back and be checked. Cle had visions of him creating a real scene. Before he could let loose one of sarcastic fusillades, Cle had him by his jacket and was yanking backwards even as his mouth was opening.

He turned to glare at her, smoothing down his silk jacket with one hand. "Cle, my dear, you are in danger of becoming an aborigine. You had best come home." His tones were frost.

"And you are in danger of getting an Australian black eye if you act up. Now for heaven's sake empty your pockets before you miss your flight!"

Jaime's keys to his house and salon were the culprits. He was the last to board the flight. Cle waited with held breath until takeoff, sure at every second that Jaime would tell the pilot to wait just one moment while he gave one more instruction to his assistant, Cle Orwell.

The return ride to downtown Sydney from the airport would have been much sweeter if Cle had been more sure of herself driving the big Mercedes. It took all her concentration to drive in the heavy traffic, so she was unable to look at the sights again. She promised herself a full tour of Sydney her first free moment. She could feel perspiration beading her lip by the time she had parked the big sedan in the space marked "Brainerd" behind the salon.

As soon as she was at her desk, Max called and asked her to come to his conference room right away. As she replaced the receiver, the phone rang again. "Cle Orwell speaking."

"It's Dev." His voice had a detached sound as though he was facing away from the phone. "Some friends have arranged for us to attend the opera this evening. I told them that I would have to check with you. Are you busy this evening?" His voice was flat.

"Ah . . . I . . ." Cle wanted to give him a haughty no but the words wouldn't come. "What is the work?"

"Madame Butterfly. I know you like Puccini."

"Yes. Yes I do . . . ah . . . I have a conference right away." She fumbled.

"All right. I'll let you go and assume you want to come. Get home early. We are invited for cocktails first. We'll have supper after the opera." Dev's voice was abrupt, then there was a buzzing in Cle's ear. The connection was broken.

If she had had time to dwell on their conversation at all, she would probably have rung him back and canceled. The first moment she had to go over it in her mind was the end of the day after Max had dropped her in front of the apartment.

She found herself laying out a rose-pink shirtwaist in silk. The severity of the style was given drama by the color and the gold-studded buttons down the front. The full skirt just touched her knee, the inverted pleats flaring whenever she moved. She was putting in antique drop-style earrings when Dev knocked at her door and opened it. She stared at him in the mirror, not moving or speaking.

"You look lovely. Are you ready?" His eyes roved over her from the hot pink peau de soie slings with the medium heel to her hair which she had coiled at her neck, a pink bone spike shoved through the chignon.

"Yes." She joined him then and they left the apartment.

"You look like Madame Butterfly with your hair in that style and with the pink needle through it."

"I have no intention of committing hara-kiri," Cle murmured as they descended in the elevator.

"I wouldn't let you." His voice held the same coolness as hers.

As he handed her into the car she couldn't stop the shiver that ran through her. If it took a thousand years, she would free herself from his hold, that emotional, spiritual upheaval she felt whenever she was near him, whenever he spoke to her.

The Porsche purred through the traffic and Cle envied how easily Dev handled the press of cars.

She cleared her throat. "Do I know the people who are attending the opera with us?"

"No, but I think you've heard me speak of Cubby Willson. He and I have been friends since Harrow."

She turned to look at him. "Oh, these aren't lawyers from a—"

"No." Dev interrupted her. "No lawyers this evening. There will be eight of us. Cubby and Lucille I know, of course. I've been in touch with them since I landed in Australia. I think Harry Blake will be here as well. Harry and I go way back. I know his wife slightly. The other couple are Australian friends of Cubby and Lucille."

"Oh." Cle felt flustered. She had armed herself against lawyers. She would have to rearm against these people. It would be harder. They all knew Dev, knew his background.

"Now don't start making a big thing out of this." His hand moved and rested on her knee. In the old days they had often driven this way. He had never seemed to be able to be with her without touching her. She knew he was only trying to comfort her but she felt tongue-tied because of the first bodily contact she had had with him in days and days.

The house was a stone building, squarish and solid. Before Cle could properly study the profusion of flowers and climbing shrubs around it, the door was open and a barrel-chested man, blond and balding, rushed through the door enveloping Dev in a bear hug.

"Finally, you old dog." The man pounded Dev on the back. "Good to see you." He stood back from a grinning Dev, still holding him by the shoulders. Dev was only slightly taller than the sandy browed giant with the pale brown eyes. "Where's your paunch, old man? Lord, will you look at mine? You would think I had the children, not Lucille."

"You look as good as when we played rugger together," Dev answered, his laugh wide, emphasizing the tiny dimples that were at each corner of his mouth. It was so long since she had seen them she felt mesmerized by them.

All at once she felt herself lifted past Dev, so that she was eye level with the chuckling Cubby. "I thought Englishmen were restrained," she gasped, laughing.

"Not Yorkshiremen," Cubby stated then gave her a big kiss full on the mouth. "So you are Cle, the beautiful Cle who has knocked Devon Carstairs out of his Italian mocassins. You *are* gorgeous. Come along. You have to meet Lucille who is eaten up with curiosity to see the woman who snagged Devon-the-Devil-with-Women." Cubby finally set her down after Dev untwined his friend from her. Still he managed to put one arm around her as he was leading her into the house. "That's what he was called at school," Cubby announced, smiling hugely when his friend told him to shut up.

She felt as though she was swept into the room on the heels of a hurricane as Cubby announced to everyone that Cle was here.

A tiny doll-like creature with carrot-red curls all over her head came up to Cle, arms outstretched. "I'm Lucille Willson and I'm married to that tropical storm." She turned from Cle to embrace Dev.

It was the warm embrace good friends exchange. Still Cle cursed the hot poker pain that lanced her insides. She was not jealous, she was not! She bit her lips. She had almost always closed her mind to Dev with any other woman. She had shut away any thoughts of the women who had been in his life before he met her. With sudden insight she realized that she was every bit as jealous and possessive as Dev had ever been. Dev had just been more open about it.

The embarrassing thought so clouded her mind that she had to have Lucille repeat the Asner's names twice. Bill and Ella, Bill and Ella. Bill was a partner with Cubby in the construction firm he had started when he and Lucille had emigrated Down Under. Harry and Tina Blake seemed very friendly.

As Cle accepted a drink she heard a scuffling sound at the door. A sandy haired toddler somewhere in the range of two to three years scurried into the room, an indulgent Cubby making a grab for a glass as the child rocked against a table. Following him came an aproned nanny cradling a round-eyed curly-haired blond in pink Dr. Dentons, a thumb in her mouth as she stared at the people.

"This is the wild part of the evening, Cle, when you meet the progeny." Cubby chuckled and opened his arms to the pink doll in the arms of the nanny. The thumb came out of the mouth and was replaced by a wide toothless grin as she lifted two chubby arms to her father.

Cle felt a sting of tears as she watched the children. She had loosely planned not to have children, knowing that the only man whose children she would want would be Dev's, but now seeing the little boy walk toward her, his slightly bow-legged walk rocking him into furniture and people alike made her insides squeeze in yearning.

He walked right up to Cle and looked at her, head cocked to one side. "I'm Jamth."

"I'm Cle," she answered, putting out her hand and bending toward James.

"My mommy is going to have 'nother baby. Nanny said 'Heaven help us,' but I'm glad. I want a brother this time. Sarah's nice but she likes her teddy bear."

"I used to have a teddy bear," Cle said. She felt Dev at her side, watching her.

James nodded sagely. "Girls is funny that way." He smiled and looked around him when everyone laughed. When he looked back, he smiled at Cle, then looked at Dev, his face solemn once more. "Are you her daddy? Mommy says you have to have a daddy to have a baby." He looked back at Cle unaware of a sputtering mother bearing down on him from behind. "Do you wanna baby?" His mother swept him high in the air but he still waited for Cle's answer.

All at once, Cle felt as if she wanted to cry. She could feel her body shake as she fought the feeling and smiled at the little boy.

Before she could answer, Dev had his arm around her. "Yes, we would like a boy just like you one day," he announced blandly, ignoring Cle's gasp of horror and her stiffened body.

Satisfied, James allowed himself to be carried from the room, announcing to his thumb sucking sister that that lady in the pretty dress was going to have a baby just like him.

Conversation immediately resumed and no one seemed to think anything of the child's words . . . but Cle. She felt coated with a stinging painful frost.

When Cubby came over laughing and apologetic about James she managed a smile and an offhand remark. Dev glossed over it by a laughing phrase, but Cle didn't really hear it. She was too busy trying to keep the torn up pieces of her insides from falling out her mouth. Dev's arm stayed tight around her for the short time they had before they all went to their cars for the drive to the opera house. Dev waved aside Cubby's invitation to ride with them, saying it would be easier if they drove themselves since their apartment was closer to the Opera House.

The drive wasn't a long one but Cle was glad that they were alone so that she had time to pull herself together.

"Cle, I could see you were shaken by James's question." Dev's voice was very low.

"Don't be silly," Cle said huskily, trying to tip her compact at an angle to catch the light. She jumped when Dev pushed a switch to light the mirror around her sun visor. "He's just a little boy. They always say things like that. He's a very cute little boy and I like his parents very much.

"Cubby is a good friend, and he married one of the best women I know." Dev looked her way for a moment. "They like you, I could tell, even though we weren't there very long."

Traffic became thick the closer they came to the beautiful building that is the pride and joy of every Sydney resident—the Opera House. Cle craned her neck to look at the sweeping lines of the building, loving the fluid grace. The artist in her sighed at the symmetry and rhythm against the night sky.

As much as she liked Puccini, Cle couldn't concentrate on the ill-starred lovers for thinking of her reactions to the little boy's words. Even "Un Bel Die," the poignant aria of love, didn't penetrate her painful reflections. She couldn't blot out the picture that kept forming in her mind of a little boy who just happened to be a miniature of Dev. Alongside a miniature Dev skipped another dark-haired child, a girl, who just happened to have really blue eyes with navy irises. She couldn't really see the singers. She flinched, blinking her eyes rapidly to clear her thoughts, but nothing seemed to help. There was Dev on stage in a naval uniform. Oh, God. Cle closed her eyes, applauding because everyone else was doing so.

"What is it, darling? Aren't you well? Do you want me to take you straight home?" Dev leaned over her as she hunched in her seat, a crease between his arching black brows, the emerald eyes appearing to probe her mind.

"What?" She tried to straighten in her seat but Dev was too close. "Oh, no, we'll go out to supper. All the plans were made."

"We're not going anywhere if you don't feel well." Dev's face had a set look as he took her arm to follow the others toward the spacious lobby.

"I'm fine. Really, I am." Cle whispered, her face tense as she tried to convince Dev, but not let the others hear what she was saying. Feeling the way she did, anything was better than going back to the apartment and being alone with Dev. She needed time to recoup, time to pull herself together.

"Did you enjoy it, Cle?" Cubby was at their side, Lucille looking bright eyed.

"*Butterfly* is my favorite opera," Cle said. "And what could be better than to hear it here." She swept her arm encompassing the beautiful lobby.

Lucille and Cubby nodded, pleased with her response. Cubby looked around him at the mass of humanity exiting the building and pursed his lips. "We had better get to the cars. We don't have far to go but we don't want to get into a traffic tangle either." He looked back at Cle. "I hope you like to dance, Cle. We have a place here that plays great disco and the big band sound from the States as well. And the food . . . ummmmm."

Cle laughed. In her peripheral vision she saw Dev make a move. "I love to dance. Just lead the way. I'm starving for food and eager to dance," she said, watching Dev pause at her side and stare down at her. She swiveled her head to look straight at Lucille and Cubby.

Cubby laughed and gestured to the others.

Dev was quiet even when they were in the car, adding to Cle's nervousness.

"What's Cubby's real name?" She tried to clear the sudden huskiness of her throat.

"Cuthbert."

Cle saw Dev's reluctant smile and sighed in relief.

"Very few people have ever called him Cuthbert." Dev chuckled. "Cubby is a very good-natured fellow . . . but not about his name. He was named for a very rich old uncle who obligingly left Cubby his money, but I don't think old Cub ever thought it was worth it." Dev threw a look her way. "Don't think this talk about Cubby will throw me off the track. When we get home I *will* press to know what's bothering you and what was bothering you while watching the opera." He parked the car after several long minutes of searching for a vacant spot. It seemed that the place that Cubby led them to was popular. "But to get back to Cubby." He said this as he helped her from the car and locked it. "His family was not poor but Cubby still made his own way. He's a very strong person."

Cle nodded. "And gentle and loving with Lucille and the children."

"Any man is gentle when he marries the love of his life. Didn't you know that, my sweet?" Dev held open the door and the blast of sound, mixing laughter and music, came at them like soft missiles. Cle was glad of the diversion so that she didn't have to respond to another one of Dev's ambiguous remarks.

The table assigned to them by the mâitre d' was a long one. It would seat everyone but it would make conversation limited to left and right neighbor and perhaps the person across the way.

Even with the air conditioning, Cle could see beads of perspiration on the faces of many of the people.

Cubby and Lucille recommended the Fettucine Alfredo and since Cle loved Italian food and north of Rome cooking in particular, she ordered it. Dev ordered Italian as well, but he ordered the scampi.

When all the orders were given, Dev rose to his feet taking her elbow. "We haven't danced in a long while and you did say you felt well. Didn't you?"

"Oh, yes." Cle felt her smile stretch her mouth. Yes, I love to dance with you, you Limey oaf, but you also know damn well what it does to me. Her smile touched the others and Cubby jumped to his feet, clutching Lucille. His forward motion carried the doll-like woman to the dance floor with her toes barely touching the floor. She shrugged at Cle, her eyes merry.

"Since I married Cub, my shoes don't wear out. Most of the time my feet are not on the ground."

Cle laughed. Then she looked up as she saw Dev watching her. "What's wrong?" She felt out of breath.

"It's been a long time since I've heard you laugh like that. I've missed it." He chuckled. "You're blushing, lady," he murmured as he swept her into his arms, the fast-paced disco music gripping them and sending their swaying bodies round the room. "God, it's been too long," Dev mumbled into her hair as he caught her twirling body close to him once more.

Cle forgot everything in the blood-sizzling joy of dancing with Dev. He made the world spin. He made the planets collide. The beat entered her brain and she felt as though she had become an extension of Dev. She looked into his face, knowing that his laughing excitement was echoed in her own face. She didn't lose a step, not a beat as his moves became more intricate. The song changed but not the beat and when others sat down, she and Dev continued.

All at once she almost faltered when she suddenly realized that people were watching them. Dev's hand squeezed her waist urging her on. She returned his smile and forgot the watchers, forgot the other people in the large room, forgot there was anyone on the earth but Dev.

With a crash of cymbals it was over and the applause rose as Dev pulled her close to his body, letting her hide her flushed face in his chest.

"You were wonderful, darling, an angel," he mumbled, smiling as he nodded and acknowledged the applause before leading her to the table.

The others at the table rose still clapping and Cle couldn't repress a beaming smile. She couldn't disguise the happiness running through her after dancing with the man she loved, the man she would always love, no matter where life took her from here.

They sat down and Dev handed her a tall, frosted glass with a mint leaf and a lime on the top. With an audible sigh of pleasure she sipped at the drink making the others laugh.

"Cle, you and Dev looked professional out there." Lucille looked admiring. "You must dance often with each other."

"We used to dance more than we have lately," Dev answered for her. "But it felt so good out there, I think we'll be doing it more often." He kissed Cle's forehead. "Don't you agree, love?" He looked at her, the glimmer deep in his eye making Cle feel as though her heart might spring from her chest.

She nodded. Of course I agree with you, damn you Dev Carstairs. I agree with anything you say. I'd hold the knife if you wanted to stab me, damn you. Cle sighed, deciding that she wasn't going to fight his magnetism tonight. Just for tonight, she would let herself sink into Dev Carstairs, let herself wallow in his strength. Just for tonight, she would let down her guard.

Supper came and Cle giggled when she attempted to let Dev have a sampling of her fettucine and he insisted that she feed him. He had never been so carefree, so boyish, she thought as she aimed the macaroni, curled around her fork at Dev's open mouth. She had to get very close to him. He steadied her with one arm around her shoulder and one hand at her waist. When his mouth closed on her fork, he made a muted ahhhhhing sound and winked at her. Then he took the fork, put it back into the pasta and began feeding her. Dev wasn't as neat as she had been, Cle was sure as she weaved this way and that to make sure he didn't drip any of the white sauce down the front of her dress.

"Dev, old chum, I haven't seen you this relaxed since we put Snedley's pet snake in the headmaster's study."

Cle laughed, pointing to Dev, saying, "He didn't, he didn't." Dev's eyes glimmered with amusement as he nodded. She laughed as Cubby described the old gentleman's hasty retreat through the window and how it had taken days to coax the terrified snake out of the chimney. In the meantime the headmaster posted a reward for information on the culprit. No one came forward.

"I wanted to." Cubby grimaced. "Because I was going out with a frizzy blonde, who . . ."

"Cubby!" Lucille hissed, pinching his arm.

"Ouch." Cubby rubbed his arm and kissed his wife. "She wasn't half the woman you are, my treasure!" He ducked his wife again then grinned at Cle. "Besides no one would have told on Dev. He has a crippling right. Took all the ribbons in boxing."

"And here, all this time I just thought you could wrestle." Cle chuckled, making Cubby roar and Dev pull her close to him.

"I've never seen you like this." Cle looked up at him surprised to find that she had spoken out loud.

"I have come to the realization that there is much about me that you don't know and that there is much that you think you know about me that is false. It's time you knew the real me . . . and all about me." Dev's face was serious, his eyes intent on her.

Cle couldn't read that unfathomable look but she reveled in the warmth. She wished this evening would never end. To hell with work tomorrow. The totally uncharacteristic thought from "dedicated Cle Orwell" made her giggle.

"Share the joke," Dev muttered as he wiped her chin, his eyes only inches from hers. He didn't even look away from her when the waiter came to clear the table.

"I was just thinking that I'll be too tired to move tomorrow . . . and I don't care."

"Good. Neither do I. We'll take the day off and go to the beach tomorrow, shall we?" Dev's voice was like melting butter, his eyes a liquid green and hot.

"Can't do that." Her voice quavered and she couldn't resist the urge to touch his face with her finger.

Dev took the finger into the side of his mouth. "I'm telling Cubby that we're leaving." He gently bit her finger sending needle sharp rays up her arm.

Cle made her goodnights and was sincere when she said that she would like to see the Willsons again.

The ride home was in silence, a warm, sharing quiet that cocooned them from the outside world. When Dev wasn't shifting the powerful Porsche, his one hand would thread through hers in a remembered gesture.

In the elevator, he caught her close to him, the throbbing pressure of him, evident in his mouth, in the hands that clasped her tight to him. He unlocked the door with one hand, his other arm still around her.

In the hallway he dropped the key on the table and turned her to face him. "Don't say no to me tonight Cle. I have to have you. It's been so long . . . too long."

Cle looked at him, then let her arms slide around his neck. She felt his heart kick into warp speed as he bent to lift her high into his arms. Long strides carried him to the door of her bedroom while Cle indulged herself by trying to kiss each pore on the face that needed shaving twice each day.

He lowered her onto the bed, his breath ragged as he unbuttoned the dress, the tremor in his hands obviously annoying him.

Cle laughed and pushed him away as she rose to a sitting position. "There. All the buttons are undone." She swung her feet to the floor and stood in front of him, feeling the adrenaline pumping under Dev's fixed stare. "Will you take off my dress?" she whispered, feeling provocative and desperate all at once. Dev was hers, if only for tonight.

He eased the dress from her body, then flung the garment behind him. He wouldn't allow her to unfasten her bra or remove her pantyhose. This he did himself with a glittering absorption that had Cle reeling. He'd always been a gentle, considerate lover. Tonight was no exception, though tonight he seemed to struggle for control.

When Cle almost finished undressing Dev, he finished himself with two violent tugs, then he lifted Cle high in his arms, letting them sink together on the bed.

"You're beautiful and you're mine." His urgent words were guttural as he pressed his face into her neck.

His mouth was everywhere on her body, his hands clenching on her in elemental need.

Cle felt her breasts fill his hands as her whole body reacted to his touch. She ached for him. He was her world. As she felt Dev hang back, she knew a sudden impatience that he didn't realize she was more than ready for him then. Her caresses had a fever in them that ignited him until he gasped.

He lifted himself over her. Their eagerness for each other was unparalleled.

Cle heard her own voice cry out to him and then she was swirled away.

CHAPTER
Eight

CLE WOKE FEELING REFRESHED, the familiar ache in her relaxed body made her sure that she had been dreaming of Dev again. Strange, she didn't recall the dream, she yawned. It was only when she stirred that she felt the weight on her body. Realization was immediate.

She turned her head to look at Dev and the night they had just spent together flooded her mind. Dev. He was really here in her bed! He held her last night and taught her new meanings of love. It had been a domino syndrome of explosions. Time after time had had woken her, his words and hands caressing, bringing her out of sleep and alert with a passion that blew away all control. They had been nitroglycerine together. Just a tremor, a feather touch, a look set them off.

She felt happy and sad. She knew she loved him more now than she ever had when they were together in New

York. It had taken the separation, her enforced denial of him to clarify what she felt for him. This was no sophisticated liaison that she could walk away from with a tear and a chin up good-bye. This was no "it was good while it lasted but" affair. This was a basic, gut-wrenching love, that was as integral to her as the left ventricle of her heart. She would die without Dev. Oh, she wouldn't end her life, she would survive, but it would be a one dimensional world, a colorless struggle. Cle could feel her throat close. She would be childless. All at once that was important to her. Before now, children had been an unimportant "maybe," something to consider, perhaps in the future...

She turned her head fully on the pillow, watching Dev, his face losing none of its character in the softness of sleep, his lips parted. All at once there was a flickering frown that ran across his face. He grunted, then the arm around Cle flexed hard until she was tighter to his form. He muttered something, seeming satisfied. She smiled and put a hand up to his unruly hair, its springiness delighting her.

She shook her head once as she lay there. No. No one else could give her a child. She wanted one that looked like Dev. If she conceived he would marry her. She knew that with a strong certainty. She closed her eyes on a spasm of pain as she recalled the words spoken by the woman at Clive's house months ago: "If he was ever forced to marry her, he would end up being very bitter." The agony brought by that memory drove her closer to Dev.

He opened his eyes, the blankness fading as he focused on her. "I thought for a moment I was dreaming. Lovely dream...but I'm addicted to the reality." His mouth feathered her cheek.

Cle knew she should stop him. After all she had to go to work. They had made love many times in the night.

But she lifted her leg and let it slide down his, her eyes only inches away from his.

"Darling, you may be a little late this morning," Dev crooned, his hand coming down to pat her hip and bring her body even closer to him. "Did I tell you that I love making love to you?"

"I think you may have mentioned it last night. Once . . . or twice . . . or three times." Cle gasped, her fingernails digging into his shoulders as his mouth homed in on her breast.

"Cle, I would want you if you didn't have a perfect body, but I'm glad you do." Dev had lifted his head looking at her with a glazed smile.

"You told me I'm too skinny again," she pouted, loving the play, welcoming the heat in her body.

He frowned for a moment. "You didn't look as good as you should, but little by little I'll have you back to perfect health again."

"I'm never sick," she muttered, not caring what words she used as Dev's mouth loved her body.

Again the crest was reached as they both strived to please each other, reinforcing what Cle already knew. There could never be anyone for her but Dev. The thought made her clutch him convulsively as they lay there in moist langor, reluctant to rise.

"Hey, what is it, angel?" Dev smiled at her, a puzzled light in his eyes.

"Nothing." Cle knew her smile was weak but she couldn't tell him her thoughts. She tried to edge away from him. "It's time I showered or I'll be late."

Dev laughed and scooped her back toward him. Then he lifted her out of the bed and strode toward the bathroom. "We'll shower together. I have missed scrubbing your back, woman."

Cle chuckled, her hands threading through that black crisp hair. "I knew you were good for something. How could I have forgotten it was scrubbing my back." She clung to him and to the moment, storing her mind with Dev.

"So I'm your slave, am I?" He laughed down at her as he let her slide down his body. "All right, your slave decrees that you have a cold shower for being so impertinent."

"Noooo, Dev," Cle squealed, trying to duck away from him. "I hate cold showers. Beast!" she squawked, trying to use him as shield in the spray.

Still laughing, he adjusted the faucet so that a warm spray ran over their skin. Dev lifted the loofah sponge and washed her in soft whirling motions which cleaned her and also excited her.

It took ages to dress because Dev kept stopping her to kiss her every other moment.

"I'd forgotten how much fun it was to dress with you." His eyes had a sensual softness that liquefied Cle's legs. His smile widened as he noted her reaction to his stare. "Your legs look so sexy in those slings . . . with just your panties and bra. My very own centerfold . . . but of course I would never let anyone photograph you like that."

"Dev, stop it," Cle wailed. "I'll never get to work."

"It's time you stopped working." He leaned down to give her a kiss, patting her derriere at the same time. "Now get dressed. I'll put out some juice."

She was so busy hurrying that she forgot to ask him what he meant when he said that about stopping work. By the time he insisted on a last kiss before they left—he to his car, she to try and catch Max who would be waiting for her in front of the building—nothing was in her mind but rushing.

Work went smoothly. She and Max huddled over some sketches she had done for the show he was having. Even though it was months away, he had wanted to see what Cle's ideas were.

"These are good Cle. I like the idea of using Alice

Springs as a background. The coolness of design in the driest spot in Australia. Nice touch." Max had patted her on the back, literally and figuratively and Cle was pleased.

They worked through the day without stopping and when Alistair Nivens came to tell her that Dev was there to pick her up, she could only stare at him. Feeling giddy with happiness because Dev was waiting for her, she tried to hurry and succeeded in only smearing her makeup. Finally she was ready.

Taking a deep breath she pushed through the double doors leading to the showroom of the salon, where Dev was waiting for her.

He had been watching the doors, lounging back against a desk. As she came through he didn't change his stance but she saw the electricity in the gaze that roved her body. There was a possessive, satisfied look there. The warm look widened into a smile that heated her body like a hot poker. Cle had the distinct feeling that her blood had indeed begun to sizzle.

"Hello." He straightened and came toward her, bending down to take her mouth with his, his reluctance to end the kiss very obvious. "Max says that you have been working like a Trojan all day." He leaned back to look at her. "I've ordered Chinese food for us. We'll have a little music, a little bird's nest soup and we'll relax. How does that sound?"

"Wonderful," Cle breathed, knowing that if he had suggested sky diving without a parachute her answer would have been the same. She was going to be alone with Dev!

Dev had to stop to pick up the food which didn't surprise Cle but when he insisted on stopping for champagne, she laughed.

"Champagne and chow mein. Lovely."

"I thought we agreed that champagne went with everything." He grinned at her as he started the car again.

"I don't remember that . . . but, still it sounds nice." She was so happy she could have floated over Sydney without benefit of balloon.

When they parked the car and began to unload, Cle protested when Dev piled the boxes higher. They weren't heavy, but she argued that she couldn't see where she was going.

"Stop complaining, love. Didn't you know with us it has to be fifty-fifty all the way?" Dev's lopsided grin made her heart thump erratically.

"It seems to me it's more like sixty-forty at the moment." She frowned at him as he added a carton of noodles to her load, then laughed as he struggled for his key and tried to juggle the parcels at the same time.

"You'll be punished, my darling jester," Dev threatened. He set the packages down with a thump. Cle stuck out her tongue, then streaked for the bedroom, laughing.

She didn't even have to decide what to wear. She had known from the moment that Dev said he had bought the food and they would be alone that she would wear the punjabis in turquoise and blue that he loved to see on her.

What imp prompted her, she would never know, but she brushed her hair until it shone then twisted it in the Oriental chignon of Madame Butterfly. Then she proceeded to take great pains with her makeup. Not even for shows had she ever donned quite as much but she was striving for an effect. Slowly the face she knew changed . . . oh, not so that it was unrecognizable but so that now it had an Eastern look to the features. The eyes had an alluring almond shape to them, the black eye liner making them tilt upward. The cheekbones seemed to be more defined, yet more doll like.

Satisfied, Cle nodded, and slipped into the punjabis. She had to gasp when she looked in the mirror again. She did look Oriental.

When she went out into the lounge area Dev was bent

over the coffee table between the two couches. He was dressed in one of the loose silk shirts that he enjoyed for leisure. They had no buttons but were wrapped around the body and tied to one side with sleeves that were full and cuffed at the wrist. This one was in a sea green that would compliment her punjabis, Cle thought gleefully as she watched him, waiting for him to notice her. His slacks were a thin silky cotton that delineated his strong lower torso, emphasizing his narrow waist and hips, his muscled thighs. He had cotton clogs on his feet and looked totally relaxed, at ease. All at once he straightened and turned toward her, a glass in his hand.

It looked as though he were going to offer the glass to her—but he didn't. For milliseconds it was as though neither of them breathed. Then he exhaled sharply, placed the glass on the table and looked back at her.

The song on the stereo seemed loud all at once. The throbbing voice seemed to come from a personal chanteuse they had hired just for the evening. And her love song was "Why Did I Choose You?"

Dev walked toward her, stopped a foot away and bowed from the waist. "You honor me, beautiful lady." His voice had a richness that made Cle's pulses throb. "Will you dance with me?"

Cle nodded, her hands still folded in front of her in the Oriental gesture of obeisance.

Dev opened her fingers one by one, kissing them.

She could not take her eyes from him as he pulled her into his arms. She knew the song changed but she had no idea what the music was as she swayed in his arms. As Dev pressed his lips to her forehead and she closed her eyes, she thought her happiness was butterfly-like—beautiful, glorious, but short lived. She shut out the future, determined to live only for the moment.

"We had better eat dinner, my lotus blossom, or we won't eat at all." His voice was a low growl in her ear.

Cle giggled and let him lead her up a step to the dining

alcove with the angled windows and beautiful view of Sydney at night. Before they sat down, they looked out the window at the traffic, at the buildings. Cle had never felt more happy.

Dev kissed her cheek. "You set the table and I'll put the food in dishes."

Cle shook her head at him, knowing she was glowing. "I'll never get used to the domestic you."

"Well, you'd better. I intend to take over the kitchen at least once a week when we're back home again." Dev patted her rear, not seeing the shadow cross her face. "Now get those place settings ready and I'll get the food." He called the last over his shoulder as he went into the kitchen.

Moving like a robot, Cle got the cutlery, glasses, and plates. Dev must have known that she was committed to staying here for two years. Surely she had mentioned it. She felt dejected. After all, what difference did it make? She was not going back to the States with Dev. It would be too hard. Misery overwhelmed her. How could she live without him? Or under these tentative conditions *with* him?

Dev brought in the food and she forced a smile. She would enjoy every second with him! *She would!* He opened the champagne with a minimal pop, and filled two glasses.

"To us." Dev toasted her.

"To us," Cle responded, striving to keep her mouth from wobbling.

The food was good and very fresh and they helped each other to vegetables, noodles, pork, assorted fruits. They ate slowly, often pausing to smile at each other.

"We are not having dessert, my lady. We're having Irish coffee," Dev announced saluting her with his champagne glass.

"I thought you always told me to be careful with booze." Cle leaned both elbows on the table, placing her chin on her clasped hands. "If I have an Irish coffee after this champagne, I'm liable to fly out the window." She grinned at him. "Besides, Englishmen don't drink Irish coffee."

"That's a base lie." Dev caught her hand and placed his mouth on the back of it.

The courtly gesture had her gasping.

"Will you be my lady, Cle?" Dev asked, his lips just above her hand, his eyes fixed on her.

"I will be your lady tonight, good sir," she murmured.

"Good. I also want you to be my lady for all my life." Dev's smile had a lazy power. "Will you do that, too?"

"Don't be silly. We always said that marriage was not for us. Don't you remember?" She felt a bubble of hurt float through her body. "Now where were we?"

Dev leaned back a little in his chair, the muscles of his face taut. "I was proposing marriage. That's where we were. Now *when* shall we marry?"

"Never." Cle reached for the champagne glass, but before she could take a sip, Dev removed it from her hand.

"Listen to me, Cle, I don't know what game you're playing, but I don't like it. We *are* getting married."

"Don't be—"

"And if you call me silly again, I won't be responsible for my actions." Dev looked grim.

"Why are you pushing to marry me now?" Cle squalled. There was a voice inside her screaming, "To hell with worries, grab him now. Marry him. For however long it lasts it will be all the happiness you will have your whole life long."

"It's time I had an heir?" Dev asked, the facetious question having a hard humor. He stood and took a tray from the sideboard. "I'll get the coffee. If I don't get out of this room for a minute, I might do something I'd regret."

"Don't talk like a fool," she shouted after him. "No

one today marries to get an heir."

There was a short silence then Dev returned to the dining alcove carrying the tray now laden with steaming coffee, cream, Irish whiskey, and a cream liqueur.

Cle watched him, her hands clenching and unclenching. "No one marries for an heir," she muttered again, glaring at him. How dared he destroy the beautiful mood! Why did he have to mention marriage and make her recall the conversation she had heard at Clive's home?

Dev threw her one acid glance then he contined to prepare the Irish coffee. A jigger of Irish whiskey, a generous measure of coffee, a small amount of cream liqueur, a generous dollop of heavy cream topped by freshly grated nutmeg. He passed one of the artistic concoctions in the crystal mug to her and she mumbled a thank you.

She sipped the coffee. It was delicious and she praised him.

"You have cream on your nose." His smile was slow in coming as he dabbed at her nose with his napkin. He leaned back in his chair. "Why are you fighting me on this, Cle? You know we're good together. What more proof do you want that we are quite solid as a team than the last year we spent together? Can you say that was bad?"

"No, I can't . . . but that was different."

Dev's chair crashed backwards as he surged to his feet. "Let's finish our coffee in the other room. We'll take care of this later."

Cle preceded him feeling heavy hearted. She didn't have too many arguments to use against him. She didn't want to tell him what she had overheard because he would overcome every reason. She knew him well enough to know that he would be furious with her for accepting such a specious argument as the conversation she had overheard, for throwing a wrench in the works. Dev would ride roughshod over anything or anybody who dared to assume what he might think or do. He would expect her to do the same, but Cle couldn't help the feeling of truth that cloaked her like doom when she had heard Clive talk to the faceless Lydia.

She sat on the couch expecting Dev to sit opposite her. He sat next to her, very close, and pulled her back next to him. "You're mad at me," Cle babbled, loving the warmth of him, feeling soothed because his chin massaged her hair.

"Am I?" Dev crooned near her ear. "I suppose I am." His arm tightened around her. "You confuse me, lady. I admit that. There's much about the inside of you that's a mystery to me. Maybe I've never even met the deep down you, but I've decided that I must try to." He sipped his coffee with one hand and massaged her neck and shoulder with the other.

"You are?" Cle swallowed, burrowing her face into his chest.

"I am."

"You're a busy man."

"Yes."

"You have business interests all over the world that need your attention."

"That's true."

"Mustn't neglect business," Cle said, her eyes blinking in pleasure at his stroking.

"Never," Dev muttered, taking tiny bites of her ear lobe. "Shall I show you something that belongs to you and that I was going to give you tonight?"

Cle tried to push away from him. "No . . . you mustn't give me anything . . . not now." There seemed to be a tiny explosion in her head. She knew what he had for her—and she couldn't even bear looking at it!

Dev held her tight, his mouth not leaving her hair as he delved into his pocket. "Easy, my angel, don't fight me. It won't do you any good." His voice velvety low, but threaded with steel. "I know you won't let me give it to you now, but I want you to see it."

"I don't want to see it." Cle gritted her teeth, squeezing her eyes shut.

"Open your eyes, love. Come on, do as I say."

"I don't have to," Cle wailed childishly.

"Cle!"

"All right . . . but I won't take it! I won't like it either!" She opened her eyes to look into his, wondering how Dev could stand her the way she was acting. She had never been childish . . . even as a child, she thought giddily. She had always been quiet, studious, obedient . . . Oh, Lord, she thought with disgust she sounded like a German Shepherd!

"Cle? Cle, will you come out of that daydream and look at this?" He maneuvered her around in his arms, so that she was facing more forward. In his free hand he held a square leather box . . . just as she'd suspected.

Tears filled her eyes. She stared at the box as though it were Pandora's. Let it be a bracelet . . . necklace . . . anything but a ring!

Dev snapped the catch and the top flew back revealing a white velvet bed. A large sapphire, rectangle in shape, lay there. It was a deep blue, multifaceted, giving off a mesmerizing fire from its depths. The setting was gold and ornate. Cle knew it was old.

"It's the Carstairs betrothal ring. Do you like it?"

"It's beautiful . . . but I could never wear it. It must be very valuable."

"Very valuable," Dev observed drily, ignoring the first remark she made. "I've had it cut to your size and cleaned. I'll keep it until you're ready to wear it."

"Is something wrong with your hearing?" Cle asked testily, twisting her head around so that she could look at him. "I'm not wearing it."

Dev looked down at her. "When you get angry with me, your eyes darken almost to navy . . . almost to the same color as the rim around your irises." His voice had a musing sound as though he were talking to himself. "I think I love your eyes best."

"Don't you ever listen to me, Dev Carstairs?" She glared up at him.

"I always listen to you, darling. You're a very interesting lady, whose opinions I value."

"Well, you don't sound . . . You value my opinions?" She studied his face to detect mockery. There was none.

"Very much so. Other than the closest colleague, I've never discussed my business more with anyone than I have with you. How often at night have we sat on the floor in front of the fire and talked with each other about what we did that day?"

"Quite often," Cle said, recalling how late it would be sometimes before they realized the time. They had rarely watched television. They were too involved with one another for such distraction. More often than not if they stayed home—and they stayed home quite often on a week night—they would listen to the stereo and talk. Yes, she did know quite a bit about Dev's business, she conceded. "But you never talked much about your family."

"My family is not as interesting as my business." Dev grinned down at her. "But if you want to know about it, ask. There are skeletons in the closet, but I won't hide them from you. For instance, my grandmother was one-quarter Irish, but my grandfather loved her anyway. She only died two years ago and I miss her yet." Dev's face was closed for a moment. "I sometimes think she was the only one of them who ever knew me."

Cle didn't move. She watched the hard muscles of his face move under the flesh because of the emotion he was feeling. "You were lonely when you were young," she burst out.

"Was I?" His eyes flashed downward like a warm

caress, "I was in Debrett's Peerage. How could I be lonely?" His voice was light, but Cle saw the shadow in his eyes.

"I would have liked to have known you when you were a boy. I'll bet you were an awful handful, into everything." She snuggled closer, sighing when his hold tightened.

"I was. Once when I was at Larren and my mother and father were traveling as they often did, my mare was ready to foal. I was afraid for her. I had nightmares that the grooms would be too busy with Father's hunters to watch over Grilla. So . . . I slipped out of bed late one night, went down the kitchen stairway, and went to the stables and brought Grilla to my room."

"You didn't!" Cle exclaimed, imagining a boy coaxing a pregnant horse up the back staircase of an Elizabethan manor house.

"I did," Dev said firmly, frowning at her laughter, his own eyes bright. "Then I had to go back down again and get straw and hay before Grilla would settle down."

"She didn't stay the night?" Cle looked at him wide eyed.

"She did and was quite content with her straw on the Aubusson carpet, so content that she foaled near dawn," Dev said, his eyes remembering, his laugh infectious. "I don't know if you've ever seen a horse foal, but sometimes they have a difficult time. Grilla didn't have a horrible time but she did have a little bit of trouble and she let me know about it. Lord, how loud her neigh was! The whole staff came running. The butler was apopletic, cook nearly fainted."

"Oh, God!" Cle trilled, hanging on to Dev. "You didn't really do this?"

"I did. Believe it. My tutor whaled me with a strap. It took days of cleaning to get the smell out of the house. My father and mother were furious. My grandmother laughed and took me to stay with her until the dust settled.

She even arranged for one of her grooms to go to Larren and care for Grilla so that I would be at peace. My father didn't dare argue with her. She would have ripped him apart and if my mother said anything, Grandmama would reduce her to tears in minutes. She was my bulwark against the world. When others would call me incorrigible, Grandmama would say I was just like her dear Willett and glare at everyone."

Tears trickled down her cheeks. "Oh, I wish I could have known her." She gulped, taking Dev's hankie from his pocket and wiping her eyes.

"You would have liked her and she would have adored you with your wild ways." Dev heaved himself from the couch, then swept Cle up and close to his chest.

"Me?" She closed her arms around his neck as though it was the most natural thing in the world to be carried to bed by Dev. "I'm not wild. I'm very sober and hard-working."

"You're wild and free and untamable and I'm glad, even though sometimes you're a trial to me."

"Monster." She bit his ear, making him flinch. "Put me down this instant."

"I'm going to . . . just as soon as we reach the bed." His eyes had a liquid emerald look and Cle forgot everything except her deep, deep love for him.

"I hope you're not tired tonight, angel. I have a feeling that I'll want to keep you awake most of the night." Dev undressed her with a sensual absorption that narrowed his eyes, gave a lazy droop to his lips, and when at last she was completely stripped caused his nostrils to flare.

"Dev, I hate it that you were lonely," Cle whispered as he lowered her to the bed.

"Then make it up to me. Keep me close to you and never let me be lonely again." Dev nuzzled her shoulder, his mouth wet and thrilling. "You're mine, Cle. You must see that."

"I do see that, Dev, but . . ."

"No buts tonight, love, just you and me together."

Cle wondered for a fleeting second if any other woman in the whole world were as lucky and knew such pleasure. Was she the only one who caught fire because one man, the only man for her, was there with her?

"Cle, my God, your hands, they're driving me crazy." Dev groaned, his body writhing next to hers.

There was such a feeling of power in knowing that she aroused Dev as much as he aroused her. It was always new for them, always the first time. Cle felt protective and alive with him, shared and alone, ecstatic and solemn. He was her man and the whole world to her.

The rocket ride to climax was an intolerable heat that warmed Cle to her soul. There could never be an ecstasy greater than that she shared with Dev. Rapture and agony fought for control of her mind and body as she clutched Dev tightly.

"Marriage would be sweet between us, love. Admit it," Dev muttered sleepily, his hands stroking her in lazy satisfaction.

"Your family would hate me." She nuzzled under his chin.

"Who cares what they think? I don't."

But you would, someday, she said to herself and sighed.

CHAPTER
Nine

DEV SEEMED TO be everywhere. He would show up just as Cle was going to take a lunch break and drive her somewhere secluded for a meal. When Cle would protest, he'd smile then kiss her cheek, and refuse to take "no" for an answer. He knew she had very little breakfast and was always in a rush in the mornings, but somehow he always contrived to have them together over juice and coffee. Dinner was a problem. If Cle said she wasn't hungry, Dev would get something from a takeout place and they would picnic, sometimes in a park, sometimes in their air-conditioned lounge. That was the worst . . . when they were alone. Dev would watch with that half smile, his eyes like an emerald brand. Almost as bad was when they were invited somewhere. If Dev were not invited, he would insist on driving her. That was rare. More and more people invited them as a couple.

When the Nivenses invited them to their beach house again, it was on the tip of Cle's tongue to decline. Then Diana said that she had mentioned it to Dev and he was delighted to accept.

"How nice," Cle observed, her voice having a hollow sound as she doodled on her drawing board and listened to Diana outline the event. The face that appeared on the paper was Dev's. Dev with horns, a tail, cloven feet, and a trident in his hand. Cle replaced the receiver on the cradle after promising Diana that they would be there. "Damn him, damn him, damn him! Why is he doing this? He's backing me into a corner and enjoying every minute of it. It would serve him right if I *did* marry him. Then his whole family might go up in atomic smoke! She could imagine a throng of Carstairs screaming their outrage at her inclusion in their illustrious family.

Then what would she do when the dust settled and Dev began to notice how poorly she fitted with his titled friends and family members. Jump in the Thames River the first chance she got! She crumpled the picture of the Lucifer-like Dev and tossed it away, refusing to dwell anymore on the situation that tortured her.

"Sydney is lovely, isn't it?" Cle said to Dev as they drove to the Niven's house on Saturday.

"A wonderful city. I hope we can visit it often in the future." Dev laughed when she glowered at him.

Cle was tight lipped.

"All right," Dev said. "Truce. We'll have a good day surfing, enjoy the company, and then go home."

Cle nodded, watching him, suspicious of his congeniality.

The surf was up! Awesome waves rolled shoreward. The cooling breeze lifted the black strands of Cle's hair and blew them into her mouth. She glowed with excitement when Alistair gestured to the beach and pointed to the boards already down there. Dev was there when she jumped to the sand. He caught her, laughing.

She couldn't have stopped the bubble of answering laughter if her life depended on it. She felt good. She always felt good with Dev.

"Stay with me," he commanded, his voice stern.

A second's rebellion died easily. "I will," she promised.

He leaned down to kiss her hard.

When Cle looked around, Diana was watching her, a knowing smile on her face. She could feel the heat in her cheeks as she pushed her board out into the water, lowered herself onto it and began to paddle out, then all thought of anything but the pulsating water left her.

Dev was patient but firm. He refused to let her take waves he thought were too strong for her, but no matter how many times she wanted to go out, he agreed.

Finally, she and Diana declared they had had enough and Max decided he would stay with the women. Then Cle had a chance to see that Dev had greatly understated his expertise on the board. He and Alistair paddled out. They were confident and sure on the boards. She couldn't help jumping to her feet when she saw Dev take the curl, riding down the tunnel of water, balancing the board, walking it, dipping it up into the curl, his body in total command. Her heart rose in her throat like a live thing as that roll of power chased Dev shoreward. When it looked as though he must fall, he corrected and stayed steady. Cle knew that Alistair had found a big wave as well but her eyes never strayed from Dev. He was bigger than the wave, bigger than the world. He filled her vision to the exclusion of all else. When his board hit the beach, she expelled the breath that until that moment, she hadn't realized she held.

His grin was for her alone, a pride in it, as though he had ridden that curl just for her.

She could feel the answering smile widen her mouth and all at once she was running toward him, arms outspread, full of joy and laughter. Dev was victorious. He had dared Neptune and he had won.

He dropped his board and caught her up in his arms, swinging her around, holding her close.

"You were wonderful out there. I thought I'd be afraid . . . and maybe I was a little." She held his head with both hands. "But I was excited, too. It felt like I was with you." Cle's tongue clove to her mouth on the words. She felt naked, unprotected, as though she had opened her skin like the pages of a book and allowed Dev to read her insides.

His face sobered. "You're always with me. I thought you knew that. No matter what I do or where I go."

Cle swallowed, letting one hand trail down his cheek.

"Hey, are you two going to cuddle all day?" Max yelled, a pouting mannequin from the salon on his arm. He waved at them. "Time for sundowners."

"Coming," Dev called back and began to carry Cle up the beach.

"Put me down," she burbled, her hands still tight around him. "I'm too heavy."

"No." He smiled down at her, the green electricity of his eyes dancing on her skin. "I like to carry you. I'll be able to carry you when you're heavier, too."

"What does that mean?" Cle was puzzled.

"Nothing." He shrugged, the shuttered look to his eyes making Cle frown. Before she could say any more, they were at the rocky base of the incline leading to the house and Dev set her on her feet. He still kept his arm tight around her, but didn't look at her as they walked toward the house.

Diana handed cold beers all around and gave Cle a seltzer with lime.

"You looked like a professional out there today, Dev," Alistair said.

Dev saluted with his beer. "You looked pretty good

yourself. This is a beautiful surfing area. I think my sisters will like it."

Cle's head snapped around. She saw the querying looks on the other faces.

"Are your sisters coming to Australia?" Max asked.

"My whole family is coming out for a visit. My two sisters, a younger brother, Roddy and my aunt and uncle Simes. I have numerous cousins but they won't be coming." Dev announced all this in bland fashion, his eyes skimming from one person to another.

Cle had the distinct feeling he was avoiding looking at her.

"Why are they all coming now?" Diana made a moue. "I suppose I'm being too curious. You needn't answer..."

"I don't mind answering." Dev took a deep draught of beer from his mug. "They are coming out to Australia because they will be attending my wedding." Dev dropped his bombshell then took another sip of beer.

Cle felt like a fish tossed from the sea onto the shore. Her mouth opened and closed but no words emerged. She wriggled in her chair, trying to force her muscles into letting her rise.

"Why you secretive old dog!" Alistair Nivens clapped him on the back. "I'll bet you're doing it because you want that Willson fellow to be your witness. Congratulations."

Diana grabbed Cle's arms pulling her upright and into an embrace. "Cle, darling, I'm so happy for you. How could you have kept it so secret? I would have been shouting from the rooftops." She rocked a lifeless Cle in her arms not seeming to notice her glazed eyes. Then Diana released her and galloped to Dev's side to give him a big hug.

Max was at Cle's side. "You look as though you didn't want Dev to tell us."

"I didn't," Cle wheezed.

"Surely you were going to ask us to attend?" Max looked offended. "Jaime will be hurt. That's true. I'm Jaime's friend and don't wish to see him hurt. That's also true . . . but surely you know that I'm your friend as well and would want to see you married." Max exhaled so sharply that his nostrils flared.

"I . . ." Cle swallowed.

Dev was there, one arm coiling around her. "You didn't want me to let the cat out of the bag, darling?" He pressed his lips to her forehead.

"These people are assuming that it's me you're going to marry . . ." Cle squeaked, wetting dry lips with her tongue.

Everyone laughed and crowded round them, appreciating Cle's little joke.

"Of course, angel. Everyone knows you're the only woman I've ever wanted to marry." Dev bent closer to her.

"Baloney," Cle muttered, her body having the sudden nervous spasms one would associate with flu.

Dev held her tighter. "She's trembling," he said to the others in general.

"I'll get tea," Diana said firmly.

"I'll get the Scotch," Alistair interjected, nodding in an even more firm way to his wife.

"Hot toddy. That's the thing," Max stated.

The three of them scattered, leaving the mannequin named Jennifer staring at Dev and Cle.

"Imagine anyone being upset by a marriage proposal," Jennifer mused, staring from Cle to Dev and back again. "It's better than some of the arrangements I've been offered." She looked back at Dev, a smile sliding across her face. "I think I'd feel different if you offered the same thing to me." Jennifer's stance changed subtly. Her tummy seemed flatter, her breasts more thrusting. She turned sideways and her derriere had a more enticing curve.

Cle could feel her body stiffen. She leaned back so that she could look through her lashes at Dev. His smile had a knowing curve to it. Cle wanted to slap wet cement all over Jennifer's lissome body, then toss her in Sydney harbor. "I'm sorry but this is not an arrangement that can be filled by volunteers." Cle's voice was chipped ice. She could feel downward look Dev was giving her but she kept her eyes on Jennifer.

The other girl shrugged. "You didn't seem too interested to me."

"Perhaps you don't know me well enough to understand my reactions," Cle ventured sweetly, her hands coming up to Dev's waist.

"Perhaps." Jennifer shrugged, then looked up at Dev, her smile coy. "But just in case she doesn't decide to pick up her option, you can always ring me at the salon. They have my address and phone number."

"I'll keep it in mind," Dev responded, amused sensuality in his voice.

Jennifer raised her brows in response, then ambled from the room in the direction that Max had taken, her bottom waggling, in what Cle thought to be a disgusting fashion.

"Do you think you might unfasten those nails of yours from my waist now?" Dev asked in a conversational way.

"You are lucky I don't perform surgery on you with them." Cle spoke through her teeth. "Actually, I think you are in dire need of a lobotomy and if I can find a rusty knife I will oblige."

"Bloodthirsty little thing, aren't you? I hope it isn't genetic. I wouldn't want to think that our children would all have that unfortunate penchant for mayhem," he crooned in her ear.

"Penchant, my aunt Maude," Cle said between gritted teeth, straining away from him, but not succeeding too well. "How dare you tell those people that we are getting married!"

"Why not? It's true. We are being married. I posted the banns at Saint George's Church two weeks ago." Dev took quick hold of Cle's one free arm, kissing the fisted fingers, his eyes alight. "I would have told you at the time but I was afraid that you would have thrown a spanner in the works."

"Damned right I would have." Cle glowered at the laughing Dev.

"Well, there you are. It would have been foolish to tell you, since you wouldn't have been at all cooperative. Would you like to know where the reception is to take place, my love?" Dev let his mouth run up and down her cheek.

Cle couldn't stop the shiver that ran through her body as his lips traveled over her cheek. "Reception?" she asked hollowly, her eyes riveted on him. "What are you talking about? There will be no reception, no wedding, no . . ."

"I couldn't agree more. I don't want the fuss either, but I'm afraid some sort of fuss will be required. Sir Reginald was custodian of my estate until I came of age and though he is a crusty curmudgeon and pompous at times, I must have him at my wedding."

"He'll hate me," Cle wailed softly, seeing in her mind's eye the look of contempt on the face of the tall, imposing admiral, Sir Reginald Simes.

"Of course he won't hate you. How could he?" Dev looked at her, a crease of impatience on his forehead. "Besides I don't know what the bloody difference his opinion will make to our life together anyway." Then a smile curved his mouth. "There is Aunt Simes, my father's sister. Aunt Margaret looks like Queen Mary . . ."

"The ship?" Cle quavered, feeling confused. Dev's laugh made her jump.

"Not the ship, love." Dev threw back his head, his laughter unfettered, just as Alistair and Diana walked back into the room followed by Max and a pouting Jennifer, whose pout lifted when she looked at Dev.

Diana and Alistair had had anxious looks on their faces but at Dev's laugh, the anxiety was replaced by relief. "Everything all right now?" Diana asked, eagerly.

"Yes." Dev was still laughing. "But I think a hot drink will be good for Cle." He sat her down and accepted a cup for her putting in more sugar than she liked, then handing it to her and watching her drink, ignoring her glare.

"I was just telling Cle about the reception we'll be having in the Yacht Club," Dev added.

Cle frowned at him but he seemed not to notice.

"Both Cle and I hope you will join us that day, both at the church and at the club," Dev finished kindly, moving his hand quickly when Cle leaned toward him with the steaming spoon she had just lifted from the cup. "Careful, darling, I know you would feel devastated if you burned me," Dev cooed to her. Then he leaned over and smoothed at the lines between her eyes. "I would hate to see those lines become permanent. You're so young to have them . . . and we don't even have children yet. Though we'll probably have them soon." Dev ignored her gasp and smiled at the others.

"Ohhhh, that's why you're marrying her. How different." Jennifer mused out loud. "I didn't think anybody did that any more. Is that coming back into fashion in the States? Shotgun weddings, I mean?"

"Oh. You, you . . ." Cle searched her angry mind for a word and came up blank.

"Don't tease her, Jen," Max insisted. "She has enough bridal nerves without worrying about that." He looked back at Cle. "You look slim as ever, love. You must let me know if you can't be in the show, you know . . ." His lips pursed, his eyes getting that faraway look. He didn't notice Dev gripping Cle's wrist as she took hold of an antique andiron Diana used as a book end and wresting it from her. "Ummm I could get Della to take your place in a pinch."

"Max!" Cle's voice had a strangled sound.

"Uhhh?" He looked back at Cle, a blank expression on his face.

"I think that Cle would like you to drop the subject," Alistair offered in a soft voice, gesturing to his wife to remain calm as she glared at Jennifer. "The reasons for Dev and Cle's marriage are their own business," he finished.

"Oh, God!" Cle felt her face contorting as she looked from one kind face to the other. If it took the rest of her life, she would pay Dev Carstairs back for this one, she vowed to herself. She found herself drinking the tea, drinking the hot toddy, drinking the Scotch. When she rose to her feet, there was a distinct wobble to her walk.

"See," Max chortled, "I knew she wasn't herself. She's staggering from the shock."

"From the alcohol, I think," Dev said kindly, one arm supporting her, even when she tried to turn away from him.

They had a barbecue meal, which at any other time, Cle would have loved. They cooked prawns wrapped in foil, and deep-water fish the same way. It was all served with a lemony butter that she could feel dribbling down her chin. As side dishes there were huge bowls of fruit and iced fruit juices. Cle's enjoyment would have been ultimate if she hadn't had to worry about the wedding and the way Jennifer looked at Dev. The whiskey she had drunk dulled the edges of her reactions so that by the end of dinner she was sure her only worry was Jennifer. Marriage to Dev was only a dream that could be put aside.

The next day she spent in bed, the combination of seafood and alcohol playing havoc with her stomach and head. Dev again assumed the role of nurse and brought her cold cloths for her head and weak tea for her stomach.

Cle wanted nothing more than to have a knock down drag out battle with him but she didn't have the strength. Even opening her eyes was an agony. "You can leave, you know. You don't have to stay with me." Cle was trying to be brave even though she felt she'd been keel hauled the length of the *Queen Mary*. Damn, why did she think of that? She did not want to remember any thing about Saturday at the Nivenses'.

"Would I desert you, my little bride-to-be?" Dev crooned to her.

"I . . . hope . . . Australia's . . . largest . . . shark . . . gets . . . you," she gasped, her head splitting. "And I would never marry a man who travels in such fast company—drinking all the time," Cle finished forlornly.

"I don't have a hangover, love," Dev pointed out, changing the cloth on her head.

"I never had such things until I met you." She groaned. "You're a bad influence. Go away."

"I'll change my ways," Dev promised, laughing. He helped her to the bathroom to shower and shampoo her hair.

"Leopards never change their spots," Cle pointed out.

"I'll join AA."

"They could help you," Cle sighed.

"Thank you." Dev leaned down to kiss her.

"Don't mention it."

They emerged from the bathroom later and Dev helped her slip into a fresh nightie. As she drifted to sleep, her last hazy awareness was that Dev had done this before, that Dev had taken care of her in many unattractive situations, that he had seen her in a more vulnerable, unprotected way than anyone in the world.

When she woke in the morning, her first thought was that her mouth had turned into a desert. Her second thought was that she had to run.

She turned on her side and looked at Dev sleeping

next to her. One of his arms was thrown back on the pillow, but he wasn't laying flat on his back. His body was bent protectively toward her.

I can't marry you, Dev, she spoke to him in her mind. I want to marry you. I want that more than anything I have ever wanted and maybe if you were anyone else, I would just grab my chance and run with it. How can I with you? She lifted her hand toward the hair falling over his forehead. She touched it lightly, not wanting to wake him. You have a responsibility, Dev, and I know you. You might think that it wouldn't bother you, but I think it would some day and if we were married for years and I saw that look in your eyes, that look that said you'd done the wrong thing, then I couldn't live with that. I couldn't lose you then. Now, I have a chance of being a little happy without you. I'll have my work . . . and my memories . . . but if we were married, I couldn't give that up. It would hurt me too much. And I can't explain any of this to you, Dev, because you would just ride down all my arguments.

She slipped out of bed and into the shower, feeling logy but purposeful. This time she wouldn't just dart away. She would make solid plans so that Dev couldn't find her. She would talk to Jaime.

Dev drove her to work. He was in a relaxed, lazy mood. When he pulled her to him, outside Max's salon, his kiss was warm, promising. "I feel damned good knowing that next week at this time your last name will be Carstairs, my darling." He let her go with one last hug. "I'll pick you up tonight. Let's get take-out food, shall we?"

"Fine." Cle smiled, reaching for him, her kiss opening on his mouth.

"Hey," Dev drawled, his hands tightening on her. "I like that. Shall we go home for an hour or two?"

Cle's pulse galloped but she shook her head. "Lots of work."

She got out of the car blindly, not looking back.

When she reached her cubicle she sat there for long moments trying to formulate a plan.

She called Jaime, knowing it would be the middle of the night for him. "Jaime? Jaime? It's Cle. Yes, I know what time it is. Yes, I know how much sleep you need. I'm in trouble. I need your help. Yes. Dev has set a wedding date. Yes. If I come back to the States, I have . . . What? What did you say?" She sat in stunned silence as Jaime spoke rapidly. His plan was amazing. Yes . . . yes I suppose you're right. If I'm married to you, Dev couldn't do a thing. But Jaime . . . I don't like to take advantage of you like this . . . Yes, I know you always said that you wanted to take care of me . . . Yes, I . . . I think it's a good idea. All right. Good-bye, Jaime."

She wasn't that lucky when she called the airlines. The soonest she could have a reservation was in five days. That was one day before the wedding date! Dev would be angry. No, Dev would be bloody furious, to put it in his words, Cle thought, holding her head in her hands.

She worked through the morning on the Alice Springs collection, amazed that any ideas could come from a mind that was bent only on escape.

She contented herself with an apple and cheese lunch and a carton of skim milk, not wanting to leave her drawing board when the sketches seemed to flow from her hands.

The phone rang when she had a big bite of apple in her mouth. She chewed and then answered. "'ello." She swallowed some.

"What the devil are you eating?" Dev laughed into the phone.

Cle swallowed the rest. "Apple. Hi."

"Hi, yourself bride-to-be. Getting nervous?"

"Are you?" Cle whispered.

"I wish I could come over there and get you and get

married right now." The sensual snarl in his voice sent Cle's temperature up. She knew she was too young for a hot flash, but she felt sunburned all through her body . . . on the inside. She heard his sigh and stiffened. Maybe he was having second thoughts. "I've just gotten a phone call from my sister Tessa. She, Sybil, and Roddy will be coming in tomorrow and are booked into the Boulevard Hotel. Lord!" Dev sighed again. "They want to go to Alice Springs. Are you laughing?"

Cle had to smile at the anguished sound of his voice. "Not really. But I'm doing some sketches for a show and it will be called the Alice Springs Collection."

"Terrific." Dev sounded like a martyr. "Tessa and Sybil will no doubt buy the whole collection. First they want to fly to Alice Springs, then drive to Ayer's Rock. God, Alistair tells me that it's a three-hundred-mile drive between those spots.

"It looks like you'll be busy this week." Cle saw a glimmer of hope. If Dev was going to be busy with his family he wouldn't notice that she was gone until she was well away.

"*We'll* be busy, my love. You are marrying me. You are marrying my family. I cannot . . . I will not entertain them alone."

"You make them sound like monsters." Cle doodled on the pad in front of her, watching Dev's face appear on the paper.

"Roddy isn't bad. My sisters are whirlwinds. You notice I didn't say my brothers-in-law were coming. They take every chance they can to get a breather from my sisters."

Cle's laugh bubbled up. "You're terrible."

"That's my girl. I thought for a moment I wasn't going to hear you laugh." His voice had a husky rasp, making Cle's nerve ends tingle. "I can't keep my mind on what I'm doing thinking about you. Don't work late tonight, please."

"I won't." Cle wanted him with a real ache.

"I have something to tell you, something I've been meaning to tell you for a long time." The voice changed. "By the way, are you wearing your glasses?"

"Yes." Cle could hear the throb in her voice. "What do you have to tell me?"

"Tonight. Keep your glasses on, love. I don't want you getting headaches. Oh, God, I definitely don't want you to have a headache tonight. Later."

Cle sat there staring into the earpiece of the phone even after the voice came on telling her that her phone was off the hook. "Dev. Dev, let me go. Let me go now," she pleaded, one fist coming up to press her mouth."I will have the strength. I will have the strength to leave you," she grated out.

That evening they were hardly in the door before Dev turned her in his arms and began making love to her. The take-out food sat on the hall table despite Cle's halfhearted protest.

Dev didn't listen. His total absorption in removing all her clothes with loving caresses and punctuated by long hypnotic kisses soon infected her. "Just think, love, we are going to have a lifetime to do this." He scooped her up into his arms, his eyes a lazy heat on her. "I've been thinking about doing this all day." He strode into their room and set her on the bed, then sank down beside her, his hands stroking down her body as he removed the last of her clothes. He leaned back to look at her body as he often did, his hands making circles on her abdomen. "Do you suppose you're pregnant? I've checked your calendar. Your period is overdue."

It always flabbergasted Cle how interested Dev was in her personally, how he had always been very caring if she had a rough menstrual period. "I'm always erratic." She shrugged, feeling odd. "Would you mind if I was?" She had a moment's indecision. Had she skipped some of her pills? Lord, yes! What if she was pregnant? A rush of happy feeling coursed through her body. Dev's baby! She would have something of Dev.

"Mind?" He kissed her navel. "I'd love it! A little girl just like you with Yankee courage and sapphire eyes." Dev's words slurred as he moved his mouth over her body, his hands urgent but gentle on her form. "Kiss me, Cle. I need you so. I want you so . . . and that's what I wanted to tell you. I need every pore of you, every fiber." Dev groaned.

Crying, not able to stem the flood, Cle kissed him.

The quiet explosion of their love deepened the aura around them, separating them from all others, lifting them away and beyond to their own plane, answering an elemental need that burned away anyone else, and other thought. For one fleeting moment, Cle was sure that she saw a sturdy little boy with Dev's eyes smiling at her and her glow intensified.

CHAPTER *Ten*

DEV'S SISTERS WERE DYNAMOS, Cle thought after the second day of being whirled by them through Sydney. When she appealed to Dev, he just told her that was one of the disadvantages of being married to him, but she would learn to cope. Roddy was a slighter edition of Dev with chestnut hair. He was enthralled by the bare breasted women who inhabited Sydney's beaches.

One day when the sisters had gone to explore Argyle Arts Center, Dev suggested to Roddy that they surf at the beach where he had taken Cle.

"I would rather go to Bondi Beach and look at all the beautiful Australian breasts," Roddy answered, grinning at Cle. "Do you go topless, sister-in-law to be?" Roddy's question was asked of Cle, but he threw quick glances at his brother as well.

"No, she doesn't," Dev answered for her, the look he gave Roddy holding hard amusement.

"You were always possessive, big brother." Roddy didn't look one bit abashed.

"I'm worse now." Dev had held Cle close to him, the smile he gave her intimate, telling her he recalled every intimate moment they had ever shared. "Would you like to go to Bondi Beach, love? After all, these are your days off. You should have some say in what we do."

"Bondi is fine," Cle answered. Anything is fine as long as you hold me, she thought, her own hand gripping his waist.

Bondi Beach was crowded even though it was a week day. Cle assumed that many people took their vacations at this time of year. It was so beautiful. The sky was vivid blue, the sands hot white, the water, blue to azure to turquoise to green. The sun was an amiable ball of fire overseeing all.

Cle was openmouthed at the bare breasts. Dev and Roddy were appreciative.

One curvey young lady was stepping backward her head in the air watching a beach ball come down toward her. Roddy didn't bother to dodge her. "Ooops! Pardon me." She grinned toothily.

Roddy's face was wreathed in smiles. "Will you marry me?"

"Oh, you English!" The girl giggled, grabbing the beach ball and running back down the beach.

"I'm emigrating," Roddy announced, looking at Dev and rolling his eyes.

Dev laughed, inclining his head and smiling when a lovely young thing spoke to him. When he bent down to spread the blanket, Cle pushed him hard enough to tumble him face down in the sand.

Stripping off her jeans, she streaked for the water, her desire to drown the blonde who had spoken to Dev prickling her mind. For two cents I'd take my own top off, she thought surface diving into a roller and doing a strong crawl through the roar of the surf. In her peripheral vision she saw a dark head next to her. Roddy. She exhaled a relieved breath and smiled at him.

"Don't get too comfortable," Roddy shouted to her and gestured with his head over his shoulder.

Cle knew what that meant. She stroked harder. Something grabbed her calf and she knew she was caught.

Dev came up underneath her, his face shiney wet under hers. "Pushing me into the sand, huh, lady? Before I get even as you Yankees say, tell me why."

"You know why!" Cle tried darting to one side, but he was there. Staring at that girl's breasts," she sputtered, a wave splashing into her mouth.

"Darling, I'm an art lover." Dev laughed.

"Ohhhh." Cle put both hands on his head and pushed with all her might. Down went Dev, but she could feel his hands on her waist, taking her with him. They wrestled underwater until he finally pulled her close, his mouth fastening to hers. They surfaced just that way.

"Could you clean it up, please." Roddy was beside them looking at them in a disgusted way. "Have you no control?"

Cle tried to pull free of Dev but he wouldn't release her.

"Wait until it happens to you, brother. Then you'll understand." Dev grinned, his eyes full of that lazy heat that made her feel as though she were running a fever. He held her in the water with a minimum of effort.

When the three of them returned to the beach, Roddy and Dev began throwing a ball. Cle felt too restless to sunbathe so she began ambling along the shore, grinning to herself as she realized that she was in a very small minority wearing a bikini top. Somehow it seemed natural to watch the other women topless but she didn't feel that she would try it. Her hand went to the knot at her neck, tightening it. If the tie didn't stop loosening, she realized she might be topless, too. She had picked up a few pieces of dried wood when she stopped to watch a young blond giant sail surfing. He came right into shore in front of her, grinning at her.

"Would you like to try?"

Cle had every intention of saying no, but all at once she found herself out on the board, flying it seemed to her. She screamed at first when it looked as though they would turn over, but then the man named Torin righted them and they veered at a right angle to the beach, went down aways then returned to the beach at a forty five degree angle all the way. Cle could hear her own shrieks of laughter as they cannoned toward the beach.

Her laughter died in her throat as she saw Dev there, arms akimbo, his facial muscles working hard.

He waded out and lifted her from the surfer. Holding her in his arms, he looked at Torin, then swung away.

"You might have given me a chance to thank him." Cle pushed away as Dev set her on her feet. The slippery tie released and Cle's bra top fell at her feet.

"Cle," Dev roared, diving for the top. "Cover yourself." He grated this as he pushed the thin top at her, then turned her around to tie it himself.

"Will you quiet down," Cle hissed at him. "People are looking. No one would have even noticed that my top had fallen if you hadn't roared like Leo the Lion."

"Damn you, Cle, that panting Viking you were sailing with couldn't take his eyes off you. Do you think I'd stand here and let him ogle your breasts?" Dev's teeth snapped together on the words.

Cle wanted to laugh at his glowering face, but she

smothered it, realizing Dev was not in a funning mood.

When Roddy urged Dev to play ball again, he said that he wanted to sunbathe with Cle for a while. Roddy shrugged and ambled away. In minutes he was playing a version of volleyball with some topless girls down the beach.

Dev lay on his stomach next to Cle. "Open your eyes, love, I know you're not sleeping."

"You'll bark at me." Cle could feel the giggle deep inside herself. She was going to milk every minute she had with him, enjoy his every breath, every word.

"You look sexy enough with your top on," Dev muttered, his mouth at her throat. "I saw the way he looked at you. I wanted to tear his head off!"

The rest of the day, she was never more than inches apart from Dev.

On the ride home Roddy said that he had never had such a great day. His brother laughed. Cle pinched Dev.

That evening, Cubby and Lucille Willson came to dinner along with Max and the Nivenses. Cle had prepared *truite en colère* with the help of the caterers. When Dev winked at her during dinner Cle heaved a sigh of relief. The dinner was going well. They had opened up the dining room table, adding all its leaves and the ten people were seated comfortably.

"Dev is telling you that the food is good," Cubby leaned over and whispered to her. "You can tell that by the frown on Sybil's face. She is fully convinced that no one can cook except the chefs at Larren and her own home. It upsets her when she has a good meal any place else."

Cle laughed, then coughed to cover it up when both Dev's sisters looked at her, brows raised.

"We went to the museum today after the Argyll Arts Center," said Sybil. "I saw a diverting display of aborigine art. I was able to get in touch with someone who owned some. I intend to buy a piece."

"You want to buy one?" Diana Nivens asked, her voice faint. "It will cost the earth."

"Yes. Forty thousand pounds." Sybil smiled round the table. Cle choked. Max and Alistair gasped.

Roddy and Dev looked at one another in irritation.

"Sister never buys shoddy, you know." Tessa picked daintily at her trout.

"If her taste were as good as her pocket book is big, her home wouldn't look like a flea market," Cubby muttered from the side of his mouth. "Both his sisters are crackers."

When Cle tried to smother her laughter behind her napkin, Lucille glared at her husband.

Sybil looked down the table at Cle, a tiny frown on her forehead. "I suppose this isn't the time to mention it, but I feel I must. Duty to the name, you understand."

"Oh, we understand." Cubby and Roddy chorused, getting a big grin from Dev and a glare from Lucille.

Sybil cleared her throat. "All children must be born at Larren." She exhaled and took a miniscule sip of Chablis, then nodded at her sister who nodded in return.

"I didn't know you were pregnanat, Cle. Nice work." Roddy beamed at a startled Cle, watching her eyes round and her cheeks redden.

"Children are nice." Cubby smiled at Cle.

"I meant, of course, after the marriage," Sybil said, her tones frosty. "We Carstairs do not recognize ah . . . er . . . the wrong side of the blanket." She inclined her head at Cle who nodded back then took a gulp of wine.

"What's the wrong side of the blanket, Cubby?" Roddy asked.

"Rough side." Cubby looked wise.

"What if your blanket is smooth on both sides?" Roddy asked, ignoring Cle's helpless glare. When she looked at Dev, he gave her a blank stare.

"Throw it away, same as you do the baby born on the wrong side..."

"Let's have coffee in the lounge." Cle surged to her feet.

For the rest of the evening, Cubby behaved. Lucille stayed within pinching distance to see that he did. She had no compunction in doing the same to Roddy when it looked as though he might get out of hand as well.

Dev persuaded Cle to play the piano for them, but when he saw her nervousness in front of his sisters, he convinced Cubby that it would be a good idea for them to sing along with her. She played all the songs that she remembered from her college days, then Roddy pushed her over on the stool and began to play the school songs that had been popular in Britain.

Dev winked at her when she looked at him, mouth agape, as he sang the bawdy songs.

As soon as Sybil and Tessa stood at the piano the songs changed and Roddy grimaced at singing "Drink To Me Only."

They sang for a long time and while Cle and Diana made coffee Lucille refereed the singing so that Dev's sisters wouldn't be too put out by Cubby's and Roddy's choices.

The next day she and Dev went to the airport to meet his aunt and uncle. Cle could see the resemblance between Roddy and Aunt Margaret. She was immediately drawn to the "crusty curmudgeon" who enveloped her in a bear hug and told her that she was probably too good for his nephew.

During the ride to the hotel, Aunt Margaret sniffed into her hankie and told Cle innumerable stories about her Devvie when he was a boy.

"He was a devil in many ways," the admiral said, sitting next to Dev in the car. "But I'm glad he won't be lonely any more. Beautiful city, what Mag?" Sir Reginald asked looking around him at Sydney bathed in glorious sunlight.

"Oh, yes, quite beautiful," Aunt Margaret said tearfully, reaching forward to touch the nape of Dev's neck. "Without my mother Dev's life would have been so lonely," she mused turning her regal head to smile at Cle seemingly unaware of the red stain running up her nephew's neck. "My brother and sister-in-law were such . . . such social people, and of course, Roddy was so much younger than Dev and the two girls so much older." She sighed. "And, of course, Reggie and I were so often posted out of the country." Her smile was tremulous. "He was such a dear."

"He was a devil. Rode my best hunter when he was only a stripling. Damned creature could have killed him." Sir Reginald glowered at his nephew. "You always had good bottom Devon. Liked that."

"Thank you, sir."

Cle could hear the affection running through Dev's words.

That evening was much of the same since just the four of them dined together.

There were long moments when Cle didn't even think about her departure for the States the next day. There were even some moments when she didn't think of her marriage that was supposed to take place on the following day . . . the marriage that would never take place.

That night when she held Dev there was desperation in her.

She had almost not gotten away for the evening flight out of Sydney. Diana and Lucille had decided to have an impromptu shower and brunch. A party spirit prevailed at the Nivenses' beach house and even Sybil and Tessa had swum in the ocean. They had shown a surprising power in the water. Roddy had explained with a grimace that they had both been on swim teams when they were younger.

"Which was, of course, before my time, dear sister-in-law. They both set great store by physical prowess." Roddy's voice took on the strident tremolo of his sister Tessa. "To have good blood lines is one thing but one must always strive for excellence in other things . . . strong of limb, bright of eye." His voice came down to normal as she laughed. He grinned at Cle. "Dev has already told them that you competed as a swimmer. They liked that. They've checked you out as though you were in the buyer's ring at horse sale." Roddy leaned down and kissed her cheek. "I told them that I thought you'd take your fences well. Gad, Cle, I hope you don't like oats."

Cle's laugh was shaky and she turned away when Roddy's gaze narrowed on her.

There were gag gifts and though Sybil's eyebrow arched over the box of disposable diapers Roddy gave Cle, most everyone else laughed.

It was while Alistair and Dev were surfing again that Cle saw her chance. Roddy was off with the admiral and the other women were resting. She called a cab and left. Her bags were packed so all she did was pick up the two suitcases and have the cabbie wait while she changed into traveling gear.

What caprice made her dress as a boy, with a cap on her head in blue denim with matching Jordache jeans and vest, she would never know! In bustling Sydney International she watched the clock as it ticked closer to departure time and thought about the people who would gather to see her marry tomorrow morning. They would be hurt . . . angry . . . puzzled and Dev would be too furious to explain.

She sighed. Here she was leaving Australia, a country that she had come to love, that she wanted to explore and rushing back to America and Jaime and she wasn't sure why . . . except she loved Dev with an all encompassing love that couldn't accept less than the same from him. She needed that love and needed it for all time and half a love would just not do.

"Hi. My name's Janie. I'm sixteen. How old are you?" The gum-chewing teen-ager had a gauche come hither look that puzzled Cle until she remembered she was dressed as a boy.

"Huh? Oh . . . ah . . . eighteen." Cle smiled, then looked away.

"Gee, that's great. I'm going back to the States. My mother lives there. My father lives here in Sydney. I don't know which I like best." She sat down next to Cle, horrifying her when she edged her very round and full bottom close.

"I'm waiting for someone . . . for my . . . uh . . ."

"For your uncle, Clem, my boy," said a richly timbered voice, then a strong hand clapped her on the back almost knocking her from the seat.

Dev!

"Glad to see me?" Dev inquired silkily straightening her askew cap and lifting her to her feet by one elbow. "Now say good-bye to your friend."

"I won't," Cle managed, trying to pry his fingers from her arm.

"Gee, I thought you were traveling back to the States." The mousy brown frizz top quivered with disappointment. She even forgot to pop her gum.

"I am . . ." Cle began.

The fingers on her arm tightened to bone-cracking level. "You can walk out of here," Dev hissed into her ear. "Or I can throw you over my shoulder and carry you that way."

"Good-bye," Cle said to frizz top, her voice weak.

No words were exchanged even after the luggage was stowed into the car and Dev wove in and out of the traffic leaving Sydney International. "How did you find me? What are you? A bloodhound?" she snapped, hating the quaver in her voice. "You can't kidnap me," she said, her voice rasping. "Jaime expects me. I'm going to marry him."

The car slewed right then left as the muscles in Dev's arms contracted spasmodically, his face having a contorted look. "You must have a great desire to be a widow." Dev's words were pushed through rock hard lips.

"Don't say such a stupid thing." Cle's voice rose half an octave. "I'm not going to marry a man who will be sorry he married me in a few years, then divorce me and leave me alone." Her voice skated higher as the old fears cystallized and came out as words. "You'll cast me off like old clothes. You'll want to marry a blueblood, someone from your own class. I know . . ." She fell silent when he threw her a murderous look.

"All that damned crap you're spouting doesn't have a chance of an ice cube in Hades in convincing me, but I'll get it out of you." His foot trounced on the accelerator making the car leap like a wild thing into the passing lane, then roar past four cars. "I'll find out what it is."

Cle opened her eyes. "I won't have to worry about marrying you, will I? You're going to smash us up on the highway."

"Live or die, Cle, you'll be doing it with me, no one else and if I ever hear of Toner coming near you, I'll take him apart and then destroy his business. I mean it." The growled words had a menace that was frightening.

"You're not serious," Cle said faintly.

"Try me, lady. You've pushed me about as far as I can be pushed. The next time you try to put me in a corner, remember that I'll come out fighting." He roared into the parking place next to their warehouse flat and turned the key. "I think there is something that you have overlooked in our relationship, my dear, Cleora." Dev wrenched the keys from the ignition and turned to face her, sallow rage making his face a frightening mask. "I will kill to keep you, my pet. I mean that. Get out of the car." The whispered words sunk through her flesh like objects dropping through quicksand. She still sat there when Dev came round to her side and opened the door then reached down to lift her two suitcases. He gestured with his head toward the door, then followed her.

There was precious little communication between them for the rest of the day. Dev told her he had canceled the dinner with his family scheduled for that evening at the King's Cross. She bristled when he told her that she should retire early since the wedding would be in the morning. She was sure that he would sleep in the other room but he just stared at her coldly when she looked surprised that he would be in her room.

"I'm just making sure you'll be at your wedding tomorrow." Dev's face had a menacing twist to it but Cle was determined that she would tell him to go to hell if he tried to touch her. When he turned on his side and went to sleep, she wanted to hit him with a shoe.

The wedding was quite beautiful and even the fact that Jaime had ranted and raved to her over the phone about going through with it didn't mar its beauty. Cle was certain that Jaime was more chagrined about her wearing a creation of Max's than he was about her marrying Dev.

Her dress was a creamy blue silk sheath that touched the floor. The neck had a narrow vee to her breasts, the points of the opening almost touching her chin. She wore orchids woven in the coronet of her hair and carried one orchid in her hand. The orchids were cream with bluish centers. Max gave her away and Diana was her attendant. Roddy was best man for his brother with Cubby standing as alternate. Lucille sat with Sir Reginald and Aunt

Margaret and kept handing her tissues.

The aisle of the small church was short, too short for Cle as she watched Dev turn to look at her as she walked toward him. All that ran through Cle's mind was what Dev had said to her in the car yesterday. "I will kill to keep you."

She never heard the words the preacher said or Dev's responses or hers. Then she was walking back down the aisle, Dev holding her arm.

The reception was in a beautiful room overlooking Sydney harbor. There was even a three piece band that played while they ate. The music was soft, dancing music. She and Dev stood to cut the cake and she smiled at the remarks made to her but she couldn't shake the feeling she was walking through a dream. She drank champagne from Dev's glass, a feeling of calm growing inside her so that not even the opaque green of his eyes jarred her.

When he led her to the floor to dance, she went willingly, feeling serene. Twice she saw Dev's head jerk toward her, but her smile never wavered. Her confidence grew and when the dance tune changed to something faster she pulled back when Dev would have led her from the floor.

"Shouldn't I have a good time at my wedding?" She smiled at him, her smile widening at his puzzled look.

"Yes, you should have a good time at your wedding." Dev's eyes narrowed as she reached for him and began gyrating to the faster beat.

She whirled around him once, laughing. "Don't just stand there. Dance." Cle felt free, her hands lifting in response to the primitive beat, her hips and breasts quivering in rhythm.

For long seconds her husband watched her, his eyes uncertain. Then he joined her, his body in powerful response to the music and to her.

Cle laughed in exultant abandon, her steps having a new lightness when Dev joined her, his intricate leading a sensual challenge that she welcomed. He took hold of her, swinging her body free then catching her back close to him, not a beat, not a step missed. Cle sensed the others had backed away and were not dancing but watching how she and Dev danced. With a roll of drums the dance ended and she was caught up in her husband's arms, his mouth going to her still smiling one. At once her own arms encircled his neck, her mouth opening under his, her tongue meeting his.

When Dev released her, his eyes speared hers, his breathing ragged, his hands still clenching at her waist.

Cle smiled at the applause, looking round at the people knowing that Dev's eyes were still fastened on her.

"Wow, sister-in-law, if you and Dev ever run out of money you can always become a dancer." Roddy chuckled as he kissed her cheek. "Now you have to dance with me."

Cle could feel the reluctance in Dev's releasing grip. "Darling," she cooed, reaching up to kiss him again, her confidence like a cascade over her body. The secret that she held inside giving her abilities she hadn't realized that she had. She whirled away in Roddy's arms, smiling at Sybil as the older woman stared at her.

Cle danced with everyone, knowing with an almighty sureness that her husband hadn't taken his eyes from her for more than a minute even when he danced with others.

She was more than willing to feed more cake to her bridegroom so that pictures could be taken and more times than not it was she who acquiesced and kissed her husband on request. As her confidence grew so did the sense that Dev's uncertainties were growing. Her sophisticated husband who handled corporations with aplomb, who was no stranger to high-powered legal battles, who had traveled in the fast lane for most of life, now stuck to her like glue, his face a puzzled mask.

Cle was sorry to leave the reception, but finally Dev was able to drag her away. She promised Sybil and Tessa that they would come to England and stay at Larren. After all, she informed them airily, it was her home now. She made dates with Cubby and Lucille and Diana and Alistair for when they returned from their honeymoon whenever that might be. She hugged Roddy and told him she was glad to be his sister-in-law.

Then once more she broke away from Dev and ran back to thank Max for her wedding dress. She was throwing kisses to all when Dev bent down and scooped her up into his arms, making the guests hoot with laughter. Cle could even see smiles on Tessa and Sybil's faces.

"What in hell is going on?" Dev deposited her on the sidewalk while he unlocked his car.

"I was enjoying my reception," Cle burbled to him after he had gone around the car and come in beside her. She reached over and let one oval fingernail course down his cheek, liking the sight of the blood running up his neck.

"I don't know what the hell is going on but I'm damned glad we're staying at the flat tonight. I don't think I could drive very far the way I'm feeling." Dev checked the traffic then let the Ferrari shoot into the traffic. They would be home in minutes.

"How are you feeling?" Cle crooned, leaning close to him, letting her one finger run down his neck.

"Cle," Dev said through his teeth, the car slewing around a corner. He almost stood on the brakes twice, his driving was so much more erratic than usual. When he parked the car in front of their place and removed the ignition key, his hand was shaking.

Cle never felt so unfettered and the slight swing to her hips as she preceded Dev into the elevator was provocative.

Dev watched her as they rose in the elevator. "If I hadn't been watching what you drank, I'd swear you were tipsy," he muttered, his eyes hot as they roved her body.

Cle strode past him into the lounge when he unlocked the door, feeling him right behind her.

"Now would you mind telling me . . ." Dev began.

Cle whirled, placing her hands on her hips, chin up. "You are in love with me," she stated in solemn tones. "Really and deeply and truly in love with me!"

Dev's throat worked as red seeped into his face. "That's hardly a state secret."

"How dare you not tell me such a thing!" She leaned forward, her good humor fading, anger in the thrust of her body. "I mean the love that's forever and beyond. I did not know you loved me like that until today. How dare you not tell me!"

Dev's eyes widened as he loosened his tie. "I thought I showed you how much in a hundred ways." His voice had a stilted sound as though he had just stepped onto alien soil.

"Baloney." Cle swallowed, torn between elation and fury as she thought of herself running from him and the possibility of not having him come for her. "You have your nerve, not telling me! Why didn't you just come out and say, 'Cle, I love you.'"

"Cle, I love you." Dev's voice was low but she was sure the words carried around Australia. "May I ask how you came to realize this at last?" Dev's voice was a rough velvet.

"While we were being married it suddenly came to me. I should have known before. You should have told me. You wasted all this time and I could punch you for that."

Dev's laugh made her shiver. "Could you, love? Do you love me?" His voice had a hard richness to it, like satin pulled over iron ore.

Cle clenched her fists and stamped her foot. "You know I do. You've known forever how I feel about you."

"You never told me," he pointed out, moving closer, his one hand lifted to her cheek.

"How could I tell you?" Cle wailed. "You would have laughed at me . . . maybe."

"I've loved you since you walked out on that runway, whirled in front of me, and I could see that perfect body underneath. I nearly killed Cecil Torrance because he was looking at you and making remarks. I wanted you so much. It took all my self control not to leap up on that runway with you, pick you up and cart you to my car and take you away." His grin was lopsided, the color in his face deepening. "I wanted to ask you to marry me that night, when I took you home from the club but we had talked and you told me how modern your outlook was. I was afraid that you would laugh at me if I urged you to marry me. Then I planned on convincing you to marry me after we slept together. I loved you so much—and more every day. I hated to leave you and go to the office."

Cle watched him, lips parted, eyes wide. "I loved you more," she whispered.

"It's not possible for a person to love anyone more than I love you." Dev's face blurred in her vision as his mouth came down to hers. "You're my life," he said against her lips. "I came to Australia with the express idea of getting you pregnant and making you marry me." Dev nuzzled her neck. "So many times in New York, I was going to throw your pills away and tell you that I didn't want to live together anymore except as man and wife." He lifted his head to look at her. "I was afraid you might tell me to leave."

"How could I?" Cle said dreamily. "It was your place."

"Was it?" Dev mumbled, his hand pulling the zipper

down the back of her dress. "I felt so married to you that it was as though everything belonged to both of us." Dev lifted his head, swallowing hard. "That's why I hated and still hate Toner. I knew he loved you, that he wanted you. It was all I could do not to kill him. When you left me, I went out of my mind. I told him that I would kill him if he didn't tell me where you were." Dev's hands clenched at her waist. "I had to find you. My life was over without you. I had to make you see that you needed me as much as I needed you."

"More." Cle leaned on him in lazy contentment as he helped her step out of her panties. She placed her lips on his bare chest, the tickling sensation of the chest hair an erotic delight. "I will never have to leave you, day or night," she bubbled as she pulled his belt from his pants and tossed it in careless fashion.

Dev carried her into the bedroom, their naked bodies overheating in their need for each other. He placed her on the bed and followed her down. "Reach under your pillow," Dev muttered, his hand having a faint tremor as it traced a path from hip to breast to knee.

Cle pouted at him, not wanting to interrupt their love play, as she pulled the paper from under the pillow and raised an inquiring eyebrow.

"It's the deed to this building. You now own this flat. Are you glad?"

Cle nodded, her eyes filling. "I'll always think that Sydney, Australia, is the most wonderful place in the world no matter where we live." Cle reached for him, letting the paper slide to the floor. "If I am pregnant now, I would be so happy. If it's a boy I want to call him Devon Sydney . . . and all the rest of those names, of course." Cle giggled, wriggling closer to him.

"Of course," Dev answered, his hands urgent on her body, the power of their need building fast. "If I have you for a thousand years, it would still be two days short of my want," Dev muttered into her ear as he lifted himself over her. The world melted away and they were alone with nothing but their love to sustain them. Nothing and no one could put that asunder.

WHAT READERS SAY ABOUT SECOND CHANCE AT LOVE

"SECOND CHANCE AT LOVE is fantastic."
—*J. L., Greenville, South Carolina**

"SECOND CHANCE AT LOVE has all the romance of the big novels."
—*L. W., Oak Grove, Missouri**

"You deserve a standing ovation!"
—*S. C., Birch Run, Michigan**

"Thank you for putting out this type of story. Love and passion have no time limits. I look forward to more of these good books."
—*E. G., Huntsville, Alabama**

"Thank you for your excellent series of books. Our book stores receive their monthly selections between the second and third week of every month. Please believe me when I say they have a frantic female calling them every day until they get your books in."
—*C. Y., Sacramento, California**

"I have become addicted to the SECOND CHANCE AT LOVE books...You can be very proud of these books....I look forward to them each month."
—*D. A., Floral City, Florida**

"I have enjoyed every one of your SECOND CHANCE AT LOVE books. Reading them is like eating potato chips, once you start you just can't stop."
—*L. S., Kenosha, Wisconsin**

"I consider your SECOND CHANCE AT LOVE books the best on the market."
—*D. S., Redmond, Washington**

*Names and addresses available upon request